THE
PARKING LOT
ATTENDANT

THE
PARKING
LOT
ATTENDANT

A Novel

NAFKOTE
TAMIRAT

Henry Holt and Company   New York

Henry Holt and Company
Publishers since 1866
175 Fifth Avenue
New York, New York 10010
www.henryholt.com

Henry Holt® and ® are registered trademarks of
Macmillan Publishing Group, LLC.

Copyright © 2018 by Nafkote Tamirat
All rights reserved.
Distributed in Canada by Raincoast Book Distribution Limited

Library of Congress Cataloging-in-Publication Data

Names: Tamirat, Nafkote, author.
Title: The parking lot attendant : a novel / Nafkote Tamirat.
Description: First edition. I New York : Henry Holt & Company, [2018]
Identifiers: LCCN 2017019274I ISBN 9781250128508 (hardcover) I
  ISBN 9781250128515 (electronic book)
Subjects: LCSH: Fathers and daughters—Fiction. I Ethiopians—Fiction.
Classification: LCC PS3620.A67 P37 2018 I DDC 813/.6—dc23
LC record available at https://lccn.loc.gov/2017019274

Our books may be purchased in bulk for promotional, educational, or
business use. Please contact your local bookseller or the Macmillan Corporate and
Premium Sales Department at (800) 221-7945, extension 5442, or by e-mail at
MacmillanSpecialMarkets@macmillan.com.

First Edition 2018

Designed by Kelly S. Too

Printed in the United States of America

1 3 5 7 9 10 8 6 4 2

This is a work of fiction. All of the characters, organizations, and events portrayed
in this novel either are products of the author's imagination or are used fictitiously.

To my grandmother who grew me with stories
To my mother who loves me with and through everything
To my uncle who gave me the courage to leave
And to my father who gave me the humor to survive it all

THE
PARKING LOT
ATTENDANT

PART I: ON THE SUBJECT OF
HOW MY FATHER FOUND US A HOME
AND I FOLLOWED HIM THERE

My father and I are the newest and least liked members of the colony on the island of B——. My first memory is of vomiting upon contact with the ginger-drenched air. When I told the others at dinner, I was informed that it happened to everyone, I was nothing special. No one has yet discovered the origins of this heady perfume, and the search gives my days a purpose that is all my own. The house provided for us is the farthest from the water, located in the deepest pocket of ginger odor, and contains not a whit of storage space. Nothing can be kept on the floor, partly because the house floods and partly because spiders will crawl into our clothing and give us boils, or so claims the Danga's letter, delivered to our door after the tense welcome ceremony.

The Danga was initially unwilling to accept us or even see

my father when he arrived a month ago. They were certain that additional people would only disrupt the equilibrium of the existing twenty. As I waited for news in our empty Boston apartment, he finally succeeded in procuring a meeting, where they hid behind a black screen set up in one of the houses, and he struggled to speak on the other side of it. He asked that we be granted a trial period, offering my womb as a sign of friendship and a tool of creation. Later, confronted by my anger, he would explain that false promises were at the heart of every negotiation.

"Do you want to become extinct? Like the Shakers?"

"We are already different. We remain still during services. We do not make furniture."

"You can do better."

"There are already children here."

"Not enough of them."

"How do you know that?"

"It's in the nature of children to not be enough."

They refused him. They barred him from seeing the other colonists, they demanded his immediate departure, they reminded him that their constitution (signed in blood by all inhabitants) authorized them to hang trespassers and throw their bodies into the sea. My father asked for three days before his execution. During those three days, he learned how to fish.

On the evening of the third, he pled for one last meeting, which eventually took place in the official residence of the Danga, all brick and cement like they still do it in Ethiopia, the crooked paisley curtains an atrocious contrast. My father sat in what seemed to be the living room; the Danga occupied an adjoining nook. Slender children served coffee, eyes riveted to the floor.

"Why can't I see your faces?"

"Most people never get this close."

"Why do you go out of your way to be so mysterious?"

"That doesn't concern you."

"I take it your decision hasn't changed."

"You are to leave tomorrow morning."

Although supposedly all members of the Danga were present, a single woman's voice responded to or posed questions. We would soon learn that it was she who acted as the Danga's spokesperson. My father hesitated only briefly.

"My daughter was friends with him."

"Who?"

"She helped Ayale with much of what happened in Boston."

"Who's Ayale? What happened in Boston?" The tone had become challenging.

He told them my name. The silence was exquisite and unbearable.

"It's because of your daughter that Ayale was almost caught." The voice had hardened.

"It's because of my daughter that it was 'almost.'"

A moment of what felt like irresolution; my father pressed on.

"We need your help, but you need ours, too."

"Go on."

"You're losing confidence."

The reply was swift.

"Vicious rumors."

"You're making this all up as you go along."

"We've been chosen."

"By whom?"

"Get out."

"The truth of the matter is that one of your own broke faith; you may not trust us, but you don't trust each other, either."

He named another name. An intake of breath from behind the curtain. My father continued.

"I can make and fix anything."

"Your daughter?" The voice sounded resigned.

"She's a storyteller. Every empire requires a good origin story: at the beginning, the people did this, the people killed that, the people spun these lies into those truths into present glory, etcetera, etcetera. She can create the legend you need for legitimacy and to make people forget."

"How do you know that we won't betray you?"

"I don't know anything. The blessing and the curse of it is, neither do you."

He sipped from his cup. The coffee was undrinkable after it got cold.

"How soon can you both move here?"

"Yesterday, if you like."

My father walked from the eastern edge of the island, where the colony is located, to the western corner, a total of forty-eight miles, where he knew there was a pay phone. By the time he called, I had rewatched *Robert Redford: Collection* and had spoken to no one but our landlord; I was afraid my father wasn't coming back.

"The money is under my bed." His voice sounded calmer than it should have.

"What did you tell them?"

"I shared some thoughts."

"Were they angry?"

"Did you send in the deferral letter?"

"There's no point."

"Just do it. I'm not going anywhere."

Twenty-one hours later, I was standing next to him at the border of the colony, wondering what I had gotten us into and if we would ever find our way back out.

The Danga's introductory letter went into minute detail regarding the routine to which everyone was expected to adhere, which gave us, at least initially, an almost shocking amount of joy. We've both excelled at procedure and have learned that when the rules are clear, from the very beginning, no one makes mistakes, and no one gets hurt. This applies to colonies, families, immigration, parking lots. Each colonist must be present for breakfast at seven in the Convocation Palace, the former counting house of B——'s last royal family, where the perpetual draftiness distracts from the perpetual lack of food. Volunteers distribute memoranda to our assigned chairs, and those who are employed leave at eight in the Land Rover with which the Danga came equipped. The rest of us clean first our own and then each other's houses, in an attempt to attain the highest levels of cleanliness and community.

At noon the workers return for lunch, always seafood and grocery store brown bread. At twelve forty-five they leave while we wash clothing and use a plaster solution that my father invented to seal cracks. We've tried to barter for whatever the natives of B—— hunt, but the locals are nobody's fools: they can see we have nothing. A Danga-approved schedule determines who will cook and tell stories each night. My father and I have yet to be asked to participate.

We eat dinner at eight, still together, always together. The Danga leads us in prayer over a cleverly tricked-out public address system, via which we can both hear and speak to them. This is followed by an hour of nothing, then bed at ten. We've been told that structure is key.

In our spare time, we write letters to embassies worldwide,

explaining our position, requesting recognition and money. Those with artistic talent create posters to accompany these letters. My father has started making busts of each colonist, which he hopes will be given places of honor in their homes. Those with business acumen concoct money-making ventures. Those with organizational know-how devise plans for how to spend our hypothetical money. There has been talk of house maintenance, the building of a hospital (we have one doctor, who promises that he can train some of us to become nurses, no problem) and a school. Everything will change when we relocate to Africa, our true land. There, we will not live under such ironclad conditions, but having freedom later means eradicating it now. This, the Danga explains, is how it has always been.

We are creating a new version of B——, every day we live in it. The Danga has struck up a deal with the B—— government, wherein we pay a monthly tax and they leave us alone. I have heard that the people of B—— are big-eyed and friendly but also that they split open their children's scalps to clean the insides, hence the stench that everyone whispers about but that I've never detected, too distracted by the ginger. The rare natives we see refuse to meet our gaze, which I prefer. I'm tired of people looking at me.

We speak exclusively in Amharic. It's difficult to ascertain where each person comes from, but the accents help distinguish ethnic backgrounds. My father and I are the only Amhara, though any superiority we might be tempted to feel is tempered by the fact of who we are. I still miss skyscrapers, Mexican food, air pollution, brunch, Ayale.

There are no birthdays here because when we were born doesn't matter. This is an indication of our rebirth along with that of our nation. Nevertheless, I've always loved my birthday, and as I approach my eighteenth year, which no one will acknowledge because my father often forgets and the others don't know, I mourn that, no matter what he says, I will never see Boston again.

My father and I have been told to await the Danga's three-month review of our progress to learn if we are to accompany the settlement on its final move. I don't dare to think what will happen if we are not.

The island of B—— is more than six hundred miles away from any known landmass in all directions. These surrounding regions, when owned by other countries, kingdoms, and principalities, in other long-ago time periods, would occasionally declare war on tiny B——, attacks which, judging from the lack of anything to gain, seem like suspicious attempts to prevent boredom. The closest neighbor to the west once declared, waged, and won a war against B—— in under two days, while B—— remained none the wiser. This is now known as the Battle for Good, another clue that the altercation held no actual purpose. One gets the feeling that these decades of on-and-off, mostly one-sided skirmishes occurred because the others knew that B—— was there and couldn't stop picking at it, the topographic equivalent of a pimple.

The settlement is situated on the easternmost portion of the island, with the western edge given over to resorts, hotels, three-tier pools, and the like. Journeys between the two sides are rare, and the Danga is pleased that we have claimed the east, tickled by the fancy that like the sun, we shall begin our rise here.

B——'s climate is defined as "subtropical," which means that it's often humid and never cold. To my mind, the best wardrobe choice would be constant nudity, which is a laugh, seeing as how the one book allowed to us so far is the Bible, in Amharic. The island has a reputation for hurricanes, but there hasn't been one since the founding of our colony, which the Danga has interpreted as God's approval, apparently forgetting that hurricanes are hardly daily occurrences and they've only been here for two years. I wonder how much Ayale knows about what they've done to his vision, and make no mistake, it was always his. Everyone else is crashing a party that they didn't even know was happening in the first place.

B—— is part of the British Commonwealth, although the last state visit occurred just before World War I. From what I've gathered, B—— enjoys the legitimacy of association with an important country, without having to deal with the usual nonsense of maintaining good relations with it. I still don't understand why B—— would agree to take us on as an official settlement, what with our treasury comfortably resting at rock bottom. (One of the colony's tenets is that we shall allow ourselves no dependence on the United States or Europe, no matter how beneficial that alliance might be.) B—— itself is, inexplicably, obscenely wealthy.

Each of our houses has been constructed using a windfall of driftwood that was discovered just north of the area we occupy. The Danga encouraged the first settlers to accept this gift from the angels, forgetting that saltwater and sand are not the best playmates for wood. Tools and nails were found on the breakfast table one morning, and the result is that our houses are full of cracks, coming apart, and, frankly, "houses" only in the loosest sense of the term. My father has been doling out minor improvements and advice, but the problems remain massive and he's no architect.

The only source of fresh water is rainfall; my father has designed and constructed two dozen water-collection vessels, which most inhabitants keep affixed to their roofs, all of which leak, rendering the project a seemingly deliberate plunge into redundancy.

It hasn't escaped my notice that while the others persist in treating me like a plague victim, my father has only to tinker with an object for ten seconds before, hey presto, he's the goddamn Messiah. I don't like that people are gravitating toward him, asking him for counsel, blatantly fucking liking him. I'm sorry, but that's *not* who we are and that's *not* what we do: we're supposed to be ignored and all the better for it. Nonetheless, he continues to betray me with his popularity. I don't know why I expected otherwise. I don't know how I could have forgotten and let myself love him so recklessly.

During my second week on the island, I woke up in the witching hour between night and day and saw the sky divided into pink, orange, and gold. The lines between each were jagged but distinct, and I realized that this probably happened all the time, I'd just been sleeping through it. It made me hope that I would have something to look forward to.

When I indulge in this crepuscular glory (the colors always differ, the patterns are sometimes less defined) it's easier to believe that I'm here by choice. It's only when the sun comes out and my father silently rises from bed that I know I have once again been fooled. More infuriating is the knowledge that come the next dawn, I'll be fooled once more.

I'm beginning to feel old.

I've never liked sand. I don't like how it gets into your clothes, your shoes, your hair, your eyebrows, your eyes. I don't like how it's nearly impossible to remove. I loathe its irritatingly unique quality of chafing body parts that were never supposed

to be exposed to its abrasive virtues in the first place. I once
read that Picasso and all the others who tried to be like him
would mix sand into their paints to achieve a certain effect.
I don't see what effect would be worth the discomfort.

The only good thing about the sand in B—— is that it's
white and, as far as it's possible for sand to enjoy this quality,
fluffy. There's something seductive about it, especially when
compared with the pebble-strewn gray-brown harshness of my
childhood. This former sand made me remember how human
hair and nails continue to grow after death; I could believe that
places like Cape Cod were the compost heaps for these perpetually elongating pieces of ourselves, to be enjoyed by children
we would never meet and who wouldn't care about us if
we did.

Our house contains a single bedroom, no closets, a small living area, four stools, and a toilet room; a showerhead is attached
to the outside by a flimsy-looking piece of tin. The kitchen
puzzles us since we're not allowed to create or participate in
individual repasts: all meals are community meals. The consequences of disobedience will be dire because all consequences
here are dire.

After dinner, my father and I usually return to our home and
sit in the growing darkness and absence of words. We have no
books because the Danga is still debating whether outside literature will encourage or stymie our own literary pursuits,
and so our hands remain idle in a manner that would have been
scorned by the women of yore who embroidered tapestries
while waiting on their ladies, waiting for witches, waiting for
changes in the moon. It was on our second night, when he mentioned missing our television, that I had him laughing with my
imitations of our favorite sitcom characters, even though I've

always been horrible at impressions. I marvel at those who have made a living out of seamlessly appearing to be someone other than themselves. I haven't done a particularly bang-up job of being me, and if I can't manage that, it seems unlikely that I'll ever do better by taking on someone else. I suspect that on the whole, I am untalented at the art of existence.

Due to my general lack of ability in the household arts, I've been put to work with the children. There are three of them, aged two, almost four, and five. I've never liked children—I'm starting to realize that I don't like a lot of things—but at least it's something I can do. The two-year-old is a champion crier but can usually be forced into submission with food, brightly colored toys, or strange mouth noises. The almost-four-year-old makes up words and definitions that seem more important than those with which I grew up; one of the first, *meskote-metfo*, means someone who is only a little bit evil, and I agreed that we must start naming the degrees of wickedness, since it's the in-between villains that we're most likely to encounter. The five-year-old builds forts and runs around with imaginary pirate bands, and so we see very little of each other.

I've developed calluses on my hands and knees from scrubbing their clothing and the stains they leave behind on the walls and floors of the houses, since they're the only ones given license to roam as they please. On the pretext of watching them, I snoop through the others' affairs, to see who's still having sex, who's reading illegally, who's keeping a journal, and whether we're in it.

When my father isn't there, the others enjoy discussing subjects that, I imagine, they hope will provoke me into revealing something of what they already seem to suspect.

"I wonder if what they say is true."

"About what?"

"About how being a taxi driver and working at a parking lot are the two most dangerous jobs in the world."

"What about firefighters?"

"I'd rather deal with a fire than a man who's about to stab me at two in the morning."

"What if it was at a different time?"

"You know what I mean."

"I heard he was funneling money out of the mission to buy cars and Lucky Charms for his whores back home."

"Why Lucky Charms?"

"They liked the taste."

This sounded dirtier than it should have.

"I heard he was half Greek."

"I've never liked Greeks. Too much oil in their food."

"Give me butter every time."

"Butter every time."

Some people speak violently against Ayale, as if they suffer from personal grievances, while others say nothing at all, their silence rendering them more conspicuous. The rest of the colony prefers to talk about our eventual relocation into paradise rather than the chaos of the past. There are a few faces in each of these camps that look familiar, but I can never get close enough to know for sure. My father is distressed by how I'm treated.

"I wish they would leave you alone."

"I don't mind. I just want to know who those people are."

"Leave it. You were manipulated, that wasn't your fault, but now let's just try to stay at peace."

"I wasn't manipulated into anything."

"Then what happened?"

I roll toward the wall and say nothing because I can no longer shut myself into my room.

My father has begun to kiss me on the forehead each night before going to sleep. I don't want to admit to him how much of a comfort it is, knowing that he's on my side, even if he's confused as to what this means and why we've ended up here. Ayale always found the notion of taking sides childish and believed it contributed to most of the troubles in the world. Nonetheless, I'd always felt that he neglected to consider the inherent comfort of someone joining forces with you. No one, including—and perhaps especially—Ayale, is strong enough to thrive alone in the world. Schools and summer camps are less about education and more about kicking off the idea of community, as a survival tactic, if nothing else. I don't mean that it isn't an important and in some ways rewarding thing, community, only that we sometimes focus so much on what it symbolizes that we forget about what it actively does for us in the present and literal world we occupy.

We usually play travel after our day duties. One person is chosen to stand in the middle of the circle, close his or her eyes, and name a place, real or imaginary. Egypt and China are especial favorites. Everyone begins to drift around the room, acting as if they're in that location. These movements slowly turn into skits where one can feign meeting the natives, buying goods, being caught in a tornado. When it becomes clear which of the skits is the best—meaning the funniest—the rest of us stop to give our full attention to the winner. This is almost always a skinny boy named Teddy who studied acting. I like how fluid his movements are, one flick of a finger naturally generating a tremor in the elbow, leading directly to a shake in the torso.

It's always strange speaking Amharic in an environment like B—— where, before us, there were none like us. I feel as though we're injecting the land with a quick shot of Ethiopian, a footfall of the Horn that will reverberate long after our colony has made the leap to Africa, where it will prosper and dominate for generations, eternity even, if we can swing it.

I sometimes hate my father for bringing me to a place where we live in a cloud of notoriety, where there are no buildings and crowds to hide behind, where my ability to restore a floor to its original unblemished state is the marker of my worth as a human being. I never tell him when these moments of rage wash over me, although he must know, for I've never been able to control my facial expressions; they reveal all that I would prefer to conceal.

I still don't understand why we're here. He insists that we have no other options, that only here will we be safe. I know I ruined everything by staying close to Ayale, but I don't understand how or why it led us to this. I don't hate my father the way I did in Boston, but the space where anger gave me strength hasn't been replaced by anything, which leads me to wonder if survival on empty can be called survival at all.

The almost-four-year-old's new word for so much nothing inside you that you can't breathe is *minimtifat*.

PART II: ON THE SUBJECT OF
WHERE WE WERE BEFORE AND WHERE
WE WERE BEFORE THAT

My father and I lived in Boston for many years, although not always together: he flew there from Addis Ababa in 1984, I was born in 1985 and lived with my mother until 1991, everything had changed by 2003, and we left forever in 2004.

He left Addis Ababa to avoid enlistment. This was his mother's doing. My father was her favorite child, and after his eldest brother was taken, she embarked upon a frantic search, scouring her network of friends, relatives, and neighbors for those who owed her favors, those who could be interpreted to owe her favors, those who knew people in America, those who knew people in Canada, those who knew people she didn't know. She went through a desperate period of inviting people over for coffee, tea, lunch, dinner, gift giving. She entertained as no one had ever entertained before: the lights were never off in her house, and when she could no longer ward off rationing with bribes, she had her servants comb the black market for electrical generators, well-scented candles, people who knew the people she had never deigned to meet during her comfortable lifetime, the unsavory sort who could pull strings and levers and papers with their oily fingers and wily ways.

After three exhausting months, my father's mother found a heretofore ignored uncle, who had a daughter, who knew a hairdresser, who was on fairly good terms with a former radio host, who currently lived in a place or a condition called "Fall River." After the obligatory calls, letters, threats, promises to God to later build cathedrals, my father was equipped with legal permission to live in America for six months. His mother trained him for what he was to do once he arrived.

"You will ask this woman about other Ethiopians in Fall River."

"I will meet these other Ethiopians and befriend them."

"You will go out with them and ask questions without seeming to ask questions."

"I will find out which of the women have green cards."

"You will marry whichever woman that is."

"I will get a green card."

"You will leave her."

"Unless I love her."

"Well."

"Then I will get papers for you and my brothers."

"But first me."

"And then we will live in America."

"We will move to California."

"Unless we love Fall River and decide to stay there."

"There is nothing better than California in America. Any American will tell you this."

"How do you know? Do you know any Americans?"

"Well."

My father's father was a soldier and died while fighting the Italians. My father's mother dedicated her life to unmaking in her son all that was, in her opinion, his father's doing. She shielded him from the unpleasant and the violent, so that while his brothers rehearsed battle games and killing sprees in the front and back gardens, my father preferred to sit at the window by his mother as she smiled benevolently upon her golden child.

My father has never liked drinking, dancing, crying (his or other people's), or fighting. He was comfortable in his discomfort with others and stuck close to the corpulent sides of his mother, who was cheered by the little stick boy she thought would never leave her. He read at a frenzied pace, and it was in this way that he knew about airplanes, falling in love, love at first sight, Latin America, Moscow, work camps in Siberia, fruit pickers in California, California itself, freedom of the press, aqueducts. My father had a great understanding of a great many things, but ultimately, it was a shallow kind of insight; he was not a boy or an adolescent or an adult who took any pleasure in real-world experience. Truth be told, it frightened the living shit out of him. In the real world, one could get hurt, one had to interact with people, one had to listen and be considerate, even of the rampant stupidity by which he was already disgusted, as early as the age of seven when he saw how the servants would cry after accidentally spilling boiling water on the floor, convinced that they had burned the dead, who had apparently taken up residence directly beneath the kitchen floorboards.

When the emperor was suffocated and the military took his power only to lovingly confer it upon Mengistu Haile Mariam,

who smashed three bottles of red paint and then began the killings, his mother feared only for her youngest. The others would
make do; they always had.

All arrangements made, my father was accompanied to the
airport by his mother. The streets were quiet even though it
was morning, and he was eating a banana, the last he would
eat until B—— because he found the size of American bananas
repulsive. When they arrived at the airport, he realized that his
mother was crying. She squeezed him to her, made the sign of
the cross three times over his face and body, pressed a damp
clump of American dollars from Lord knows whom into his
hand, and then saw him into the boarding line, where they had
to separate. As my father settled into his window seat and
accepted the complimentary headphones, he reflected upon his
mother. Her makeup had clotted where her tears had run down
her face. There had been hair coming out of her moles, which
made a half-circle on her left cheek. The growing distance
between them soothed him.

When he arrived at Logan Airport, he was met by the former radio host, who had replaced her teeth with dentures so
brilliant that my father still believes they were the catalyst for
the sudden deterioration of his until-then perfect eyesight. She
had a white husband named Sam, who hugged him. This agi-
tated my father so badly that he had trouble forming sentences
for the rest of the baggage claim and car ride ordeal, which
was fine because Sam had a lot to say about highways, Sam
Adams ("No relation, ha, ha"), Quincy Market, the race question ("Because it *is* a question"), and the Common. They brought
him to a neat white house in a place that made him think of
wilderness and suicide. Decades later, upon first seeing Fall
River, I would have an identical reaction; the haunted evil of
the place is not an easy one to forget. They asked him if he was

hungry, and my father said no. He was sure that he could never be hungry in front of them. The former radio host finally asked him if he spoke English, and he said yes.

They found a job for my father as an elevator boy at a nearby hotel. Later he would move on to being a cab driver but would be fired for falling asleep at the wheel. It was fall now, and he couldn't understand why everyone was going on and on about the leaves changing color; it was beautiful to be sure, but of more immediate import was that he was never warm, not even by accident. When winter came, and with it the worst snowfall in two decades, my father prayed for the first time in his life: if God took away the snow, he would stop smoking. He's still ready to give it up once God starts pulling his weight. Everything is a two-way street, he often reminds me, not least because he knows I hate that expression.

With a month left on his visa, he still hadn't met any of the green card–carrying girls for whom he'd been coached. The former radio host didn't have any Ethiopian friends, her friends were Sam and his friends, and my father became practiced in the art of slipping into the house unnoticed and running upstairs to his room, where he would smoke and fry hot dogs on the Bunsen burner he had smuggled up there to avoid meals with them. The Ethiopian girls he met through work could see that he was green and laughed at the way he dressed and talked. He was only too glad to be left alone, but he didn't want to go back. He bore no love for Fall River, town of dust and depression, but at the same time, he didn't want to return to his mother or Addis Ababa. He had become indifferent, his letters perfunctory, often no more than three lines. He was tired of where he came from: whenever he smelled trash in Fall River, he recognized the ubiquitous stench of home, and this shamed him. I've never understood how this happened to him, and all he will say is that any love he felt for mother and country was washed away by the snow.

He met the woman who would be my mother on the Commuter Rail: he was going to Brookline to see a movie and she was a legal American resident, thanks to a distant uncle's connections. He now had a favorite movie theater and a favorite pizza place. He liked the movie theater because it showed Spanish and Indian movies, and he liked the pizza place because it was next door. It was snowing on this April day, with Boston's usual genius for weather patterns designed to cause the greatest amount of human anguish. He was wearing a denim jacket that fit him perfectly, because he requires this quality from all his clothing. (My father's wardrobe is minuscule, especially compared to those of other grown men; he is a petite human being.) My mother was wearing a dress whose color he no longer remembers. They were sitting two seats apart on the train. He asked if she was Ethiopian, she said yes, she left. A week later, they saw each other again. He asked if she liked movies, she said yes—I've noted that my mother's role in these early stories is one of constant affirmation but he abstains from comment—they saw *Mother India* together, he treated her to pizza, she left. This began a month-long period of seeing each other almost every day, barring their erratic work schedules and my father's equally erratic withdrawals of affection.

Mid-month, my mother confessed that she was pregnant; it was his, and she didn't want an abortion. My father said he didn't want an abortion either, he wanted to stay by her side, to marry her—tomorrow if she wasn't too busy—so that he could stay forever. The marriage was conducted two days later in a small civil ceremony, where the former radio host and her husband were witnesses, smiling serenely for the entirety of the ten minutes. My mother cried, the flowers were fake, and no pictures remain because someone forgot the disposable camera in the park that served as a backdrop for the post-nuptial photographs. Soon after, my father paid ninety dollars and received a brand-spanking-new green card. He then ditched Fall River, leaving a note and some cash for the former radio host and Sam—they would relocate to California, where she would star in an ill-conceived Ethiopian soap opera that was supposed to revive her long-stagnant career—and moved to a tiny apartment in Roxbury. My mother moved in with him. Around her eighth month, my father left and didn't come back for six years.

To be fair, he had a lot to deal with. He hadn't seen his family for the longest period of time in his life, he was barely twenty, facing fatherhood, and stuck with a woman whose last name he sometimes forgot. He didn't like Roxbury, he didn't like children, he didn't like America. I understand. I really fucking do.

I lived with my mother for the first six years of my life. I've inherited her tight black curls, which have started falling out since I moved to B——, and her unmitigated love for Robert Redford. We moved from Roxbury to an attic in Dorchester, then a basement in Brighton, which we believed was giving me chronic earaches, until a doctor discovered that I'd stuck a stud earring into my ear canal, no big deal. My mother never spoke about my father except to bemoan how just like him I was when I did something wrong. He would later uphold this tradition, attributing my evil tendencies to my mother's mysterious genetic pool. Taken together, it would seem that my lineage could be traced back to the two most morally polluted families in Ethiopia.

I remember that I loved my mother, in that I was happy to see her and disappointed when she went to one of her three jobs and I'd be left with the inevitable next-door spinster. My mother rarely laughed, but when she did, she went all out. She would get on a scale only if I let her hold me at the same time. When my father came back, we were in Scituate, Massachusetts, in a house my mother was taking care of for the summer, which meant that we didn't touch anything for fear of breakage and wreckage. I still don't know how he found us. He came in, she gasped, and I was glad for the distraction: Scituate sucks if you don't like boating and scallops.

"How are you? It's been a long time."

My father is understatement personified.

"Who are you?"

"Your father."

"Oh."

"What are you doing here?" My mother's voice signaled a slow and shaken recovery.

"I came to see how you were doing. If you needed any help."

"Get out."

"I regret what happened. You have no idea."

"I truly don't. Get out."

"Let me help; it's the least I can do."

"Have I ever asked you for help?"

"Of course not, but that makes it better, doesn't it? You're not asking for charity, it's just me offering to do what I should have done this whole time." He sounded exhausted.

"Did you just now remember that you had a daughter?"

"I've been thinking about you both for a while."

He cautiously smiled at me; I didn't return the gesture.

"Where have you been?"

"It's not important."

"As long as you had a good reason."

"I'm sorry. I'm so sorry. I can never make it up to you, I know, but can I try? Can you let me try?"

"Get out."

He did just that. My mother started to talk about movies and mixed tapes and walks and cold shoulders, all while sitting on the floor. I understood that she was talking for her sake, not mine. A week later, he came back and the scene replayed itself. That time, after he had left, my mother asked me what I thought of my father, and I said, Not much. When he came a week after that, my mother had been gone for two days and I understood that I would never be allowed to have two parents; it would always be a relay race where the baton you had to deliver to the next person was me and the distance between players was nearly infinite, almost the span of a lifetime. I accepted without question my father's invitation to live with him.

From when I was six and a half to seventeen, we lived in a basement apartment that was unlike the basement apartment I had shared with my mother, in that it didn't flood, the landlord had a healthy amount of respect for humanity, and it never smelled like anything because we didn't cook anything that smelled. Our meals were cereal, pasta or macaroni—my father said there was no difference between the two, I asked why did they taste different then, he said they didn't unless I could taste shapes, and this was my first clue that I might be extraordinary— grilled cheese for me, roast beef for him. Once in a while, we went to Legal Sea Foods, where at sixteen, I unofficially became the oldest Bostonian to sample shrimp for the first time. I had had to work up the courage to partake of something that looked so naked.

As I flew to B——, I thought only of my mother; she had

always wanted to be an airline stewardess, but during the reign of Haile Selassie, there were weight, height, and beauty requirements, and she was declared too short. I mourned for her loss, which felt connected to my own. I think I would be less surprised than my father if she were to eventually find her way to us here, at last.

On the Subject of How We Met Ayale

On my fifteenth birthday, my father gave me permission to travel to and from school on my own. This news was delivered as a gift-wrapped-with-trust privilege, but it didn't escape me that this also meant he no longer had to drop me off or pick me up. I didn't mind. I knew that he needed to be alone and still for as long and as frequently as possible.

My father worked in various public high schools, fixing mechanical mishaps that could blossom into full-on catastrophes at any moment. He liked this job because it required almost zero contact with other human beings. An administrator would call into the service whose employ he was in and, when my father arrived, would recount the nature of the issue by repeating phrases that included, but were not limited to, "it wasn't my fault," "it just *happened*," "maybe we should replace the whole damn thing." My father would nod and wait patiently until left alone to determine what had actually occurred.

Despite long hours alone in his car, on the job, in the car again, my father still had to contend with the fact that he had a live person to feed, clothe, and sign report cards for. Weekends were torture; I could see it in his face. He would stare helplessly as I moved around the small space, asking if we could go to the movies, the park, someplace that served food I liked, which was a rare thing. He wouldn't let me out alone because as much as he wished he could put me to sleep for specific hours of the day, he never could have lived with the guilt of something happening to me. We are similar in this way: by caring too much about what might happen in the future, we end up caring not enough in the present, too worn out to maintain that kind of attention, no matter how genuine. On those long-ago weekends we would sit in silence in the apartment, reading or watching sitcoms on our small television set (he didn't encourage laughter but could stand it if I insisted). I would follow his progress as he heated up coffee or smoked and wonder how it was possible that we were here, together, in this place.

On the birthday of my transport liberation, we went to the arboretum. He sat on a bench, I halfheartedly biked up and down a few paths, we had a slice each of the Carvel cake that had been melting next to him, because he'd forgotten that I was too old for ice cream cake, we went home, he presented me with a T pass for the month, we watched the only Robert Redford movie he could stand (*Three Days of the Condor*, a classic), we went to bed.

Public transportation made punctuality a thing of the past since the truth of tardy trains and delayed buses was irrefutable. After school, I would go to Jamaica Plain to explore dusty thrift stores and brunch-all-day cafés, sneak into movies at Copley, watch pretty waifs at the Common perform original songs available on the CDs in their open guitar cases. I learned how to navigate the city in which I had been living for more than a decade. I was confused by the intersection of Tremont and Tremont; I watched men kiss on the mouth in the South End, but my father said that I must have made a mistake; I ate Vietnamese food in Chinatown, which made me sneeze; I got a free ticket to the Wilbur Theatre's production of *Hamlet*, which the *Globe* called unconventional because the lead was fat but thank God he was British.

It was a Friday afternoon when I exited the Park Street station, eyeing the hot pretzel carts, for which I had no money because my allowance never lasted past Wednesday. I had reached the parking lot near the hat store from which my classmate Seth Taschen would later be banned when he politely asked the saleswoman if they sold hats. I was just about to double back when Amharic stopped me.

"On the one hand, he wanted his mother to like her, but on the other hand, he wanted the girl to like *him*."

"Muslims are ruthless."

"Pretty, though."

"Doesn't matter now."

"Why not?"

Four heads swiveled toward me to identify the source of the question before pivoting back to a fifth man, who was still watching.

"Because he's dead," this last said.

He was wearing a stained sweat suit, the same shade as the booth against which he leaned, his face this side of perfect. The others lit one cigarette off the last, furtively flashing looks at the speaker before beaming their gazes back down. I felt embarrassed by my interruption, at having forced someone I didn't even know to pin down and call out mortality. I didn't feel sad. I don't remember feeling sadness at that point. I watched things happen to me, adjusted myself, and resisted reflection until my mind relented and let me live blindly once more. Sadness would come later, in never-ending and expanding waves, as if my psyche was punishing me for all the years I'd dodged.

"What's your name?"

I told him.

"That's an important name."

"So they tell me."

I hadn't yet discovered the phenomenon by which Ethiopians recognize fellow Ethiopians by face and manner alone; I might have actually believed my parents and myself to be the only Ethiopians in the world. The concept of "Ethiopia" seemed too fantastical to entertain as anything but a lovely origin story. I perhaps even thought this man was a mind reader, a prophet. I wasn't entirely wrong.

"What happened to him?"

"Kassahun? Wrong place, wrong time is what they're saying."

"Who?"

He slid the *Metro* out from underneath his armpit. Five lines about Kassahun Beyene, age twenty-three, newly arrived from Gondar, non-drinker. Immediately after was a more substantial piece about an Allston divorcée who swore there was an ancient Native American settlement below her hedges.

"How are his drinking habits relevant?"

"I suppose everything counts when it comes to murder."

"I didn't know about him."

He tossed the paper to one of his friends, who caught it and seemed pleased that he had.

"Most people don't. Bigger papers didn't seem overly concerned."

"That's kind of sad."

He laughed. "Isn't it? You get used to it, though."

"What?"

"Objective reporting." He looked over my shoulder. "Are you by yourself?"

"Yes, but I'm going to meet my father soon."

"Who's that?"

I gave his name. He eyed the others, who promptly supplied the mutely requested information.

"Thin."

"Mechanic. Or something."

"Addis Ababa, his mother knew Mengistu."

"Been here a while, doesn't go out."

"Had a green-card wife, no sign of her now."

The man absorbed these facts without taking his eyes off me, while I stood there, stunned at how much they knew. This was my first encounter with the unofficial intelligence network that includes all Ethiopians in any given locale. The minute someone leaves the borders of his or her adopted state, it's like they've vanished as far as the remaining inhabitants are concerned. This is particularly apt if they move to Washington, D.C., or L.A., where our people tend to get devoured by the sheer amount of homeland.

"Where do you go to school?"

I told him. He looked impressed.

"What are your favorite subjects?"

"English and history. I hate math."

"You still do well in it?"

"Yes."

"Good."

One of the men, dark and steeped in stale smoke, asked if I knew what an Achilles' heel was. When I defined it, the men nodded appreciatively.

"A real scholar."

This came from the apparent leader, and though I didn't understand why, it meant so much to me that he might believe it.

"What is a square root?"

"Can decimals have square roots?"

"Who is Napoleon III? Careful, that might be a trick question."

"What is more important, the body or the soul?"

"What is virtue?"

"Do you have a boyfriend?"

Laughter for the first time, in an interrogation I found I was enjoying.

"What's your name?" I asked.

They laughed even harder before the man by the booth silenced them with a look.

"Ayale."

"He's famous."

"Everyone knows him."

"I don't."

Ayale smiled.

"Admission of ignorance is the first step to gaining real knowledge."

"I have to go now."

"Come back soon, anytime during normal business hours. Tell your father that he's welcome, too: anyone who creates a genuine scholar in this day and age is a friend of mine."

"Thank you."

I escaped, almost running to Government Center, where

I took the next train home. I tried to do my homework as if nothing had happened, only to strike out when my fidgeting knocked my father's toolbox onto the floor, where he was carrying out his weekly polishing. He looked at me, aghast. I braced myself for rebuke, but he merely began retrieving the casualties. I made as if to help, but he shook his head.

"Do you know someone named Kassahun Beyene?"

My surprise when he nodded made him laugh.

"How? No, but really: *how*?"

He kept chuckling as he examined a gleaming monkey wrench.

"Well, if it's the one I know, his father worked for the same cab company that I did."

I told him what I'd heard. When I'd finished, his face looked as if someone had scooped out everything inside, leaving only a flexible shell.

"His father must be devastated," he whispered. "To lose a child . . . unthinkable."

"I'm sorry."

"How did you find out?"

I explained.

"Are you sure it was really Ayale?"

"I mean, I've never met or heard of him before, but everyone else seemed convinced."

The hollows under his eyes and below his cheekbones seemed more pinched than usual as he got up and began heating water on the stove, tools forgotten.

"Are you hungry yet?"

"Wait . . . that's it?"

"What do you mean?"

"What are you going to do about Kassahun?"

"What do you expect me to do?"

He seemed furious, and though circumstances would soon prove that I was anything *but* the most observant, even I could tell that his anger was meant for someone else.

"When are you going to see Ayale?"

"Why would I go see him?" he shot back.

He was just snapping for snaps' sake now.

"He invited you!"

He gave me a small smile and nothing else.

"How about tomorrow? Can we go see him tomorrow?"

"Tomorrow's Saturday."

"So?"

"He only works on weekdays."

"How do you know?"

"Ayale *is* a famous man."

"Famous for what?"

"For being where he shouldn't be and disappearing from where he should."

He refused to say anything more, busying himself with a box of ziti, pretending he couldn't hear any additional questions. I finally left it; I didn't want to pester him to the point where he'd decide I was to never see Ayale again, not as long as I was living under his roof. Furthermore, if such a decree were to be issued, I knew I'd have to disobey.

The weekend passed uneventfully, and on Monday, I found myself taking more copious notes than ever before, listening to everything my teachers said, searching for tidbits of information to pass along to Ayale as a sign of how each day brought me closer to wisdom. It didn't bother me that I sat with the unpopular Asian girls at lunch—all rejects from all races were relegated to their table—and I was unimpressed by the newest tattoo acquired by the boy who yearned to be Goth enough to sit at the Goth table. I was above all this. A scholar had to be, in order to better observe the masses, ponder self-created theories, scoff at the notion that life followed the maxims of our school's Statement of Vision: Good Citizenship, Kindness, Honesty, Character, Art, Sports, Teamwork, Success!

In my last-period study hall, lulled into drowsiness by the rhythmic snores of the monitor, I saw my father in a new light: perhaps he, too, was embarked upon this path of solitary intellect. We all knew the man could unclog drains and reanimate lifeless pieces of heavy-duty machinery with the best of them, but perhaps, concealed behind his curt responses and taciturn companionship, he was generating theories that he thought too mind-blowing for the world and the century into which he had been born. I wondered if he realized that I, his sole progeny, had inherited his burden, that it was I who would be compelled to carry on the mantle of brilliance once he had departed for other, lovelier shores.

I went straight to Ayale's lot after school, where I posited that *Tess of the d'Urbervilles* was less a novel, and more the pathetic swan song of an imbecilic weakling. He asked me if I had read a lot of Thomas Hardy. I was surprised that he knew who he was and then ashamed. Ayale noticed, I think, but didn't say anything.

"Did you tell your father that I'd like to really meet him?"

"What do you mean by 'really'? Have you met before? I thought you didn't know him at all."

Ayale patted me approvingly.

"I'm glad you caught that, good listening. Keep your ears open for inflection, tone shift, odd word usage. It will tell you everything you need to know about the person you're dealing with."

I was so delighted that I forgot to pursue my line of questioning. I watched as Ayale talked to customers, mostly older white women at that time of day, wives who no longer worked because they didn't need the money, who volunteered at urban youth centers in order to fill the otherwise idle hours between when their husbands left for their in-name-only directorships and when they returned with a bottle of something that Jean at the wine shop had promised was the best the Loire Valley had to offer. I've never understood how much money one must accrue in order to be certain that one no longer needs any more. Even after a windfall of frozen boiler systems, my father still had to save for when work would fall off around the school holidays. The difficulty with money wasn't earning it but controlling it.

Ayale had an enormous wad of cash that he kept in the back pocket of his pants. It was this lump that he added to and withdrew from as he accepted payment and doled out change. He barely looked down at what he was doing, laughing and gesturing with abandon, and yet, if you watched closely, his attention never strayed from the precious cargo he carried under the bulk of his fleece jacket. One of his favorite topics was his luck at having escaped the plague of office work and its accompanying tortures: the ties that choked, the bosses who hovered, the cigarettes that were forbidden, the buttons that constrained, unlike the twin blessings of zippers and drawstrings.

The location of the lot was ideal for escaping unwanted—i.e., unpaid—notice, surrounded as it was by an uneven ring of massive glass buildings, all starkly contrasting with the filthy square of the lot, whose lines demarcating parking spaces had become so faded that they barely counted. Because of their angles, many of these structures didn't reflect the lot, and later, when I couldn't bring myself to leave Ayale's side, I would sit in the attendant's booth and stare through its window at the building directly in front, unable to see myself or the people around me. I imagined scenarios where the lot was a magic box that no one could see into but from which we saw and judged everything. The accumulated dirt and cigarette ash of the parking area gave off a unique stink. If I could do it all again, I would.

It was five P.M. when Ayale went into the attendant's booth and closed the door. He emerged minutes later carrying two yellow manila envelopes with names and figures written across them in fine black pen. Ayale always bought the same brand of pen and could abide black ink alone. Blue drove him into a rage.

"I'll give you a ride home if you show me the way."

Thanks to my recent habit of idle exploration, I didn't hesitate. He drove expertly, never speeding up to overcompensate for previous hesitations, using every single one of the mirrors and, what's more, using them correctly. When we arrived at my building, I got out and thanked him. At that moment, my father rose from the stoop and stepped forward, zipping his navy blue jacket up to his Adam's apple. Ayale peered out of the passenger-side window, smiled, and offered his hand to shake. My father took it after the tiniest moment of seeming like he might refuse it, like he might detest Ayale with all of his heart. Ayale told him that I had been very helpful, I had finished my homework, he was lucky to have such a wonderful daughter, it was nice, so very nice, to meet him.

"Do you have any children—"

I could tell he wanted to give Ayale a title, at least the traditional *Ato*, but Ayale laughed too hard to let him finish.

"Everyone calls me Ayale. I don't think I could take a sudden surge in respectability; it might kill me."

Ayale smiled as my father finally, almost grudgingly, chuckled.

"I don't have any children. Luckily, it's only too late for us men when we die, isn't that right?"

"That's what they say."

"I've always wanted a daughter . . ." Ayale trailed off. I had never heard anyone sound wistful before. He recovered quickly.

"I'll see you both soon?"

My father nodded, and I kissed Ayale on both cheeks before he drove off, coming to a halt at the corner stop sign.

"Had you met him before?" I asked my father.

"Only heard of him."

His tone was abrupt, forbidding further comment. As he walked behind me along the hallway, I kept turning to look at him, trying to slow down the military pace he'd set, but the obscurity never left his features, and his insistent speed never lessened. With the door closed behind us, he put on the kettle, still not looking at me.

"Do you see my khakis on the back of the chair?"

"Yes."

"Take the belt off."

I didn't understand. I handed it to him. It was black leather and surprisingly heavy.

"I'm going to beat you."

The announcement sounded mislaid in the stuffiness of the room. I stared at him, confused, as he turned on the fan. It didn't help.

"But . . . why?"

"You were late coming home. You didn't call to tell me where you were. I've been worried sick. I went over to the school. I went to all the hospitals that I could think of. I bet you didn't even think about me, not once. You must have passed so many pay phones. You always remember to call. You could have asked Ayale. He's the kind that has a cell phone."

Each sentence was a right hook to my gut; later, I was surprised to not find any bruises.

"I'm sorry! It's the first time! I won't do it again!"

It seems silly now that I was so scared, hardly able to speak for the tears that were choking me. After all, he wasn't wrong: these were the rules, and the rules had been broken. I was guilty; I had to suffer the consequences. I can only offer up the explanation that he had never told me what punishment would ensue from going against his word. I had simply always done as told, a gag reflex, a lack of imagination.

He allowed me to finish my babbling and turned the kettle off when it began to whine its dirge of completion. He poured himself a mug of tea and set it on the countertop. When I had tired myself out into whimpering, he told me to pull down my jeans. I did. He told me to lean against the couch, which served as the dividing line between the living room and the kitchen. I did. In that eternal moment between the first downstroke of the belt and the *crack-snap* sound it made upon contact with my skin, I closed my eyes. When I screamed, I opened them and saw that his mug was no longer steaming; I remember thinking it was the fastest-cooling tea I had ever seen.

Five strokes later, he was done. He told me to pull up my jeans and go to the bathroom, where I discovered that I had wet myself. I threw my clothing on the floor and then took a long bath, the kind I used to take when I lived with my mother. Unlike my father, she didn't care or perhaps didn't understand the concepts of heating bills and water conservation. He didn't knock on the door or shout from the kitchen to get out before I melted all my skin off, like he usually did. I heard nothing when I finally slunk into my room to put on my pajamas.

When I came back out, he was watching television. Without turning, he said that my portion of macaroni and cheese was still hot if I wanted it, and I realized that I was ravenous. He reached out for his interminable tea, and I saw that he was having trouble grasping the handle, his hands shaking. I passed the mug to him. He took it, still not turning, and I helped myself. This was before restaurants saw macaroni and cheese as something to specialize in, charging ridiculous prices because it was covered with bread crumbs, bacon, gorgonzola-wrapped apple slices, diamond flecks, mother-of-pearl crustaceans. Real macaroni and cheese will always come from a blue-and-yellow box, with a separate packet of bright orange to be squeezed onto the tubes of pasta, a fluorescent mayonnaise. When I had finished, he stopped me before I went to my room.

"Don't ever make me do that again."

I nodded.

On the Subject of the Right of Kings

I couldn't make out if Ayale was extraordinarily wealthy or just putting on a front of extraordinary wealth. He didn't seem to own a credit card; when clients asked for the nearest ATM, he'd hesitate before pointing in the direction with the most stores. It was as if he'd never been inside a bank. He used cash exclusively, pulling out bills from rubber-banded rolls of hundreds, fifties, twenties, tens, always with a bemused smile, as if he, too, was puzzled by these hidden centers of abundance.

He often overestimated how much was needed for an excursion. He'd sometimes hand me two fifties and a five for the movies, and if I protested, he'd murmur, For popcorn, as if I might be asked to replenish Eastern Europe's supply. He hated it when people tried to pay him back.

Ayale's parking lot was not the largest in Boston. The maximum legal capacity of forty cars had been painted onto two gigantic signs by the entrance, so there could be no room for ambiguity and, thus, for mistakes. What was not mentioned was that these forty cars could fit into their designated forty spaces only if they were midsize sedans or smaller. Anything bigger, and the number dropped significantly.

I would sometimes happen upon Ayale, in mid-whisper, with one or more of the other attendants, who would scatter upon my arrival. When I asked what was going on, he would gravely explain that they had been discussing my beauty and were put to shame by its unexpected appearance in their sordid midst. While I smirked, he would quiz me on what I had read in that day's *Globe*.

Ayale's supervision became crucial to the way I saw the world. I still find myself quoting from articles, debates, and essays that were explained, contested, or provided by him. Fiction was the only area in which he faltered, claiming that it existed for the privileged alone, those who were so wealthy that they could erect glass walls to shut out reality, to reflect back upon them their own smooth exteriors, allowing them to concoct peoples, situations, and places that were more to their liking. But couldn't reality itself be a collective fiction? I earnestly asked. Ayale just as earnestly noted that such observations were best shared with the other hippies at school, exclusively.

At the beginning, Ayale hid his insults behind a smoke screen of funny. My father once noted that if Ayale took the time to find friends closer to his own level of intelligence, he'd soon be left with no one; they'd ditch him after the first round of verbal offenses, too well concealed to wound any of his usual minions. Upon seeing my expression, my father kindly added that he was just talking about the other attendants—one could hardly call me a friend. This only made it worse.

For the first few months of our acquaintanceship, I tried to space out my visits to Ayale's lot; I was mortified lest he suspect that I actively looked forward to his company. Everyone knew what happened to people who clung too hard: they were left with nothing. Unasked, I would provide reasons for my being in the area: a doctor's appointment, the only dry cleaner my father trusted, a friend who'd canceled at the last minute, yet another school report on Trinity Church ("Make sure you include how the whole thing's a French plot to get rid of America," rasped one parking lot client, who wouldn't leave until she'd seen that I'd written down her exact words). He accepted each and every one of these explanations, immediately drawing me into whatever article, book, or conversation he'd been engrossed in before my arrival. After seeing how he barely heard my excuses—I was there because I was supposed to be—I stopped saying anything. I simply started on my homework in the booth or in his unlocked car, waiting for him to take notice of my presence.

If it was a slow day, he'd let me drive the expensive cars around the lot. I am a skittish driver, sweaty and sure of death behind the wheel, a fear that intensified after an attendant from across town collided with a brick wall in his own lot. Ayale assured me the attendant had been prone to drinking, but I felt far from comforted as I pulled off shaky three-point turns in my first Mercedes. We agreed that Jaguars were uncomfortable. It was more that I agreed with him.

Ayale's preferred eating style was to wolf down as much as possible with as large a group as could be mustered. He ate alone only when hunger overtook his ability to find someone with whom to satiate it; solitary consumption made food taste like something shameful. He had a highly developed palate for junk food but was also an exacting connoisseur of quality, pinpointing when the meat wasn't the right grade or the lettuce in his Hilltop Steakhouse salad was on the verge of wilting. This was perhaps linked to his formidable sense of smell; some mocked him for his fussiness, even in the lot, hardly a model of cleanliness. What they failed to see was that Ayale's nose picked up not on unpleasant smells but, rather, unexpected ones. When he sniffed out the putrid banana at the bottom of Tadele's gym bag, hidden under a mountain of sweaty boxing gear, this was less due to distaste and more to his awareness that something was present which should not have been. Ayale ordered Tadele to dump out his bag's contents right then, to the delight of the small audience of men who were as much staples of the lot as the cars themselves. I barely smiled, eyes fixed on the humiliation in Tadele's face. Ayale's silent glare seemed to indicate that, like the banana, something had gone bad in Tadele himself. The two stayed locked in the booth for an hour; then Tadele left, and I never saw him again.

Ayale would often stand in the street as his attendants drove around the lot, directing them with shouted commands and large gestures as they assembled themselves into angled horizontals and verticals, ignoring the white lines intended to provide simple but firm guidance for vehicle placement. I didn't understand— surely this was the opposite of what they were meant to do?— but didn't ask. Not knowing means you don't belong.

Ayale liked giving presents when presents weren't expected. Christmas was a wash, but if he saw a sweater that matched the color of your eyes, it was yours.

He was able to identify 100 percent Italian wool, on sight. I was given to understand that he had a closet full of unworn elegance, all of it awaiting the day sartorial splendor would be required. Each Sunday was dedicated to trying on selected items, in order to confirm their fit and suitability. The solemnity with which this ceremony was conducted seemed no less than that which accompanied the preparation of Holy Communion. Ayale may have been a holier man than anyone realized, although his gods and laws were unknown to the rest of us.

I once heard a woman's testimonial about visiting a prison in Ethiopia immediately after the Red Terror. She described the horrid conditions, the boredom that drove the young guards to unpredictable violence, how profoundly her heart went out to those who had spent the prime of their lives within those walls. She mentioned how easy it was to identify the sons and relations of the former emperor. According to her, the blood of Haile Selassie set these individuals apart so that something, perhaps the knowledge of being wronged, of deserving better, emanated from their bodies. Even mired in that squalor, they could never be mistaken for just another prisoner. She called it "an invisible but blazing coat of arms, imprinted upon the very matter of their bodies."

At the time, I wanted to strangle her: another white woman using Ethiopia to measure the length and strength of her heart-strings. I don't feel that way anymore. I've realized that since meeting Ayale, I, too, have used Ethiopia and my Ethiopianness to measure my worth, to feel that I had proof of being different from or better than others. At least that woman *did* something. She got herself to a place that must have been as much unlike her home as anything else, looked at death with both eyes open, and lived to tell the tale. I just puffed myself up with borrowed grandeur.

About a year after meeting Ayale, I was lying in bed and got to thinking about her again. I was sifting through what I remembered from her talk when I shot up and sat for a long time, looking at nothing. Was it all just romantic fancy? Could royalty be distinguished by the imperceptible? Had anyone else thought about this? Had *everyone* else thought about this? Was I the sole person who hadn't grasped how natural our gravitation toward Ayale was, marked as he was by the sign of the emperor, bestowed upon those whom God Himself has elected? I lay back. This was absurd; boredom and adolescence were loosening my grip on reality. I didn't even *believe* in God.

But did my believing in something render it true? Doesn't the truth remain the truth, regardless of what I think?

I realized that be it sooner, be it later, Ayale was liable to drive me out of my goddamn mind.

On the Subject of
How My Father and I Came to
Learn About B—

Two streets over from our apartment, there lived a monk in a wretched house that seemed forgotten by the Boston Housing Authority and civilization itself. It had been blue in better days but was now filthy white, with navy patches that I sometimes thought were where the house was finally and irrevocably losing feeling. It was a one-story, with a porch that had become the resting place for the tops of the overgrown weeds in the yard. Half of the stairs leading up to the porch were missing something which was crucial to the essential nature of being a stair, and one of the banisters had been removed.

We'd assumed that no one could possibly be living in such a wreck. There were never any lights on—at least, none that were visible from the outside—and we'd yet to see someone enter or exit. My father believed it condemned: whatever enigma had made the previous owners leave in such a hurry had clearly required immediate evacuation. I didn't like the look or feel of the place. I closed my eyes and held my breath when we passed it in the car, something I had never done anywhere else, even when passing a cemetery. I liked cemeteries when the library was closed and I wanted a quiet place to read. I didn't like cemeteries when a Baptist funeral party had gotten there first.

Two Sundays after I'd met Ayale, my father decided that we should go to church. These holy impulses came upon him about twice a year. He had explained to me, carefully, that he believed in God, of course he did, but he didn't believe in churchgoing, at least not for himself.

"Too much hypocrisy. Most of the people you see there every Sunday are the worst sinners that you'll ever meet, you mark my words."

I tried to believe in God when I was a child but soon gave up. On the scant Sundays that church was suggested, I would shrug into one of my dresses, which my father kept impeccably ironed. We would arrive and instantly separate, since men and women sit apart from each other in the Ethiopian Orthodox church, a system I'd initially believed he'd orchestrated so that he wouldn't have to sit with me. I'd choose a seat in the farthest-back row (the church was never full, as people had overnight shifts at the parking lot, the twenty-four-hour Dunkin' Donuts, the 7-Eleven) and promptly fall asleep. I would be nudged awake by one of the unbearable altar boys, who would glare as he shook his velvet umbrella for a donation. I would fork over the dollar with which my father had entrusted me before going to his side of the church (and it was always "his side" for me, never "the men's side"), the boy in question would look disgusted, I would discreetly check for drool.

On this particular Sunday, as I tried to find a comfortable spot in my empty pew, the priest went up to the lectern and said a few words about God, the importance of attending church, and the importance of giving money to the church even if one couldn't attend. (I sleepily wondered if he'd had to hold himself back from saying that giving money would be preferable to empty-handed attendance.) Then the priest (who bore the cross of a heavy Oromo accent and a mostly Amhara congregation) announced that today's sermon would be given by a young monk, newly arrived from Jerusalem. A murmur arose from a group of women in front of me. I tried to sit up as the monk took the priest's place. He thanked the priest, the congregation, the walls, for their indulgence of a poor man who had so little to offer by way of enlightenment. I was drifting off again when he finally began.

It wasn't so much that he had new information to offer as that he was funny, even while discussing the Bible, a defiantly uncomical text. True, the funniest parts seemed unintentional, but one still had to give points for energy. His was a pleasantly deep voice, a far cry from the priest's uncertain stutter, and when he had finished, my father turned and raised his eyebrows at me.

As usual, we didn't stay for the food that the women had prepared, and as we walked toward our car, we heard footsteps behind us. Turning, we saw the monk, attempting to run but failing, apparently because no one had ever taught him how to do so. He appeared to be mimicking the motions of a rabbit on a treadmill.

"Good morning!"

He beamed as he shook hands with first my father and then me. We mumbled our replies, unused to speaking to other people. My father thought to thank him for his sermon. He waved this away with an embarrassed laugh.

"I'm sure it's clear that I have no learning. My family was too poor to put my brothers and me through school, and when my mother died, we all had to separate and find our own ways of moving ahead in the world. I haven't seen anyone from my family since I was a child."

We stared.

"Have you always lived in Jerusalem?" asked my father, after what I knew he hoped to be the appropriate amount of time to let pass after an admission of devastating loneliness.

"I've lived there for ten years now."

The monk alone seemed completely at ease, perhaps because his condition was anything but news to him.

"Do you like Jerusalem?"

"I have never felt it is where I am meant to stay, but I believe it was where I was meant to be."

"But . . . do you like it?"

"As much as one can love a place to which one has been destined, one has been sent, one has been flung in order to call together, to love, to teach, to be."

My father sighed almost inaudibly and I, too, felt we were getting nowhere fast with this charismatic caller, lover, teacher, be-er. Almost as one, we did a half-turn toward our car, the universal sign that one is about ready to leave a conversation. Obviously, this monk had spent too much time wandering around Jerusalem to learn anything about the universe, never mind its signals. He remained rooted to the spot, smiling benignly, giving not the slightest indication that he had any intention of leaving this piece of ground. Less so as one, we made our respective half-turns back toward him.

"I actually wanted to speak to you about something," the monk began. "I noticed your daughter—I assume she's your daughter—because there aren't many young girls in the congregation."

My father's face underwent a minor spasm.

"I must commend you, sir, for understanding the irreplaceable importance of regular churchgoing in any child's development. I've often said that parents should pray that their child be raised *within* the church, that their child develop a talent *for* the church—for going to church *is* a talent—because a child that knows and stays with the church, that child will never fall, he will never fail, he will never falter. That's what your father has given you, young lady. Never forget that."

The monk shook his hand again. My father looked nauseated.

"So, as I watched your daughter and how quiet and attentive she was, I realized that she should join our latest project, one that's barely off the ground! It's an exciting thing, to be so crucial to a program of this kind, a founding member, you might say. So I'm asking you both to consider this idea and your extended and extensive participation in it."

My father and I waited.

"What's the project?" I finally asked.

"Of course! How silly! I meant to say it all but, as always, I got to the ending part a little faster than the beginning part, and then, sometimes, the endings get so interesting and I forget to explain how we got there, because it's so much more exciting to see where we'll end up, don't you agree?"

My father politely replied that he hadn't the slightest idea.

"We're putting together a young adult choir, and we thought your daughter would be an excellent preliminary member."

He smiled wider than he had yet.

"I can't sing."

"I'm sure that's not true."

"She really can't sing."

"I'm sure she could learn."

"I don't have time."

"We don't have time."

"Rehearsals would only be once a week."

"Impossible."

"I'm in a play and I do—"

"Volunteering."

"At a soup kitchen."

"Which is very far."

"In Worcester."

"Salem."

"Salem, I meant."

"I wish she could."

"I wish I could."

"But we have to go now."

"We're late. They're going to kill us."

The monk looked stricken, both at our refusal and at how we might be murdered.

"I'm sorry to hear this, but of course I understand. Everyone here is so busy, it's not like Jerusalem."

"Not at all."

"Jerusalem is the opposite of Boston."

"Yeah."

"I miss how people would linger over coffee for hours and hours after church. It was like church was everywhere and at every point in our lives. It was like we never left church."

This proved too much for my father. He lurched toward the car, I waved at the monk, we fell in and couldn't stop laughing. Instead of heading straight to our subterranean home, he turned toward Copley, parked in front of a café I had passed on my recent wanderings, and we had brunch, in a restaurant, for the first time: sausage and eggs for my father, blueberry pancakes and bacon for me.

We didn't return to church for the rest of the month, or any Sunday after that, until we had to leave. We brunched instead. My orders varied widely: from blueberry pancakes, I leaned toward waffles, then breakfast burritos, then nothing for a while because I was trying something different, then fruit because I was trying something healthy, then bacon-and-fried-egg sandwiches when I didn't give a fuck anymore, then blueberry pancakes when I calmed down. My father never erred from the path of sausage and eggs. We willfully made our lives the opposite of Jerusalem: every Sunday was a determined remembrance of *not* being in church, of *not* carrying it with us wherever we went.

He would tell me stories during those brunches. Not long ones, nor true ones, I suspect, but ones that involved his family, his classmates, and the time he threw his co-worker's weed into a sewer because he hadn't understood. For those few hours a week, he solidified into a real person with needs and preferences, one who would forgive and accept all that I said and did because we were kin. Only at brunch could I see him as someone who would stay. At all other times, I prepared myself for his inevitable departure, after which there would be no more parents: I would be alone.

Soon after we had made the monk's zealous acquaintance, we began to run into him almost everywhere we went, separately and together. We saw him at grocery stores, pharmacies, trying to decipher the English titles at movie theaters, walking toward Coolidge Corner, looking as if he had no idea why or how he had arrived at this precise moment of his life. It was around this time that we found out he was our neighbor, a nerve-racking discovery.

After a week of discussing the rather fantastical happenstance of a perpetually appearing monk in our midst, I came home to discover my father looking trapped on the living room couch while the monk spoke excitedly about freeing some animals but killing the others. He stopped when he noticed my entrance, and my father took what seemed to be his first breath in hours. The monk rose with his cross upheld for me to kiss, and as usual I fumbled and ended up pecking it farther down than those with physical and spiritual grace should. The monk smiled benevolently as I sank down onto the couch next to my father, who was gazing with longing at a lighter on the coffee table. He started when I patted him on the back.

"Now, my child, I have to ask you something, something that I already asked *him* and which *he* got wrong." His eyes were twinkling, I swear to God, twinkling like they do in books. "So I hope that you can save the day. Do you feel up to the challenge?"

He helped himself to a dusty box of cookies that my father had bought at a long-ago school fundraiser. They were chalk-colored and had evil-looking red goo in their centers. The monk couldn't get enough of them. He was knocking himself out. The corners of his mouth were stained with red goo.

"Um, yes. I do. Feel up to it."

"Excellent. Here it is: what do you think of music?"

"What kind of music?"

"Any kind."

"Including church music?"

"That's not music; that's God in a different way." The monk was stern.

"Including country?"

"What's country?"

"Don't ask him about country," snapped my father.

"It doesn't matter. I like music."

"Ha! Of course you do! I'm not asking you that, though. I'm asking what you think of music itself, what qualities you would attribute to it: is it inherently good or bad, does a different set of standards apply? Take your time, my daughter. Have a cookie—it will help your brain."

"How," muttered my father.

"Sugar makes the brain work faster."

"What?"

"Science," said the monk.

"I guess music is good because it can make whatever mood you're in more intense. So if you're sad and you listen to sad music, it can actually help you feel better because you're stuffing yourself with sadness."

The monk looked at me pityingly.

"You are wrong, my child."

"Excuse me?"

"Music is a sin. That's all there is to it."

"Is this a joke?"

"No." My father sounded mournful.

"My child, you say that music makes you feel whatever you're feeling more strongly? Be it sadness, anger, happiness, love, etcetera. I'm right about what you meant?"

"I guess, basically, sure. So what's the problem?"

"My child, how could this be anything but a sin? How can we possibly keep our minds on God, on Jesus, on our own salvation if we're too busy focusing on nonsense lyrics and noises which make us feel too emotional to do anything but listen?

Without tranquility in heart, body, and mind, there is no real prayer—never forget that, my child."

"He's serious?"

"He's serious." My father crossed his arms.

Over the next two hours, the monk revealed many mysteries. These included: why Muslims should never sit near our icons, why Catholics were condemned to unnatural sexual relations, why coffee was a sin, what the Jews knew that we were still learning, why women should wear hats in extreme heat, what nail cutting meant for a weekly taker of Holy Communion. There was nothing we could do except invite him to dinner, which he happily accepted. My father sent me to the corner store for bread and milk and, when I returned, used the pretext of forgotten butter to make his escape and smoke as much as he could stand. When he returned, whorls of smoke radiated from his nostrils.

My father made two servings of ziti and a serving of linguini, before combining them with two brands of tomato sauce. I toasted the bread. The monk ate most of the food. We started dropping hints about going to bed: tomorrow was a busy day, we said, talking wildly of dentist appointments, hospital visits, school shopping in Natick, coat repairs. The monk heard nothing, only thoughtfully asked if we had anything sweet on the premises. I was given another dollar for a chocolate bar. When the monk had finished, he continued to sit, staring intently at a point in front of his nose that was of sudden and extreme fascination.

"I often wonder about B——."

His voice went soft on the unfamiliar word, as if it were being tugged from somewhere deep within. Perhaps he'd been yearning to say it since he'd met us but couldn't risk us not understanding; after all, we were the heathens who'd opted for

THE PARKING LOT ATTENDANT   55

church nowhere because we hadn't the constitution for church everywhere.

"What do you wonder about it? What is it?" My father was one decibel below screaming.

The monk looked up in surprise.

"It's an island."

"I've never heard of it."

"That's impossible."

"And yet, here we are."

The monk returned to looking directly in front of him.

"I wonder if it's as beautiful for our people as they say it is."

"I bet it's beautiful for everyone. Islands are always beautiful."

"You know that I sometimes regret not going when I had the chance?"

"What's stopping you?"

"And the natives like us, you know. We look like them, we're used to that kind of weather, we're patient, we're not malicious."

"I need you to stop acting like anyone besides you knows what you're talking about."

I was surprised by my father's gentleness. The monk nodded but then hesitated.

"Can I have a cigarette?"

My father fumbled with the pack as he handed it off, but he couldn't resist teasing.

"I'm sure it's a sin."

"Even Jesus had His moments of doubt."

He and my father puffed in silence before he cleared his throat and began.

"While I was in Jerusalem, a woman came with instructions to see us from her priest in Minnesota. Our monastery was known for its healers—not me, but many of the older ones—and she had a condition which made it impossible to sit down. No one could diagnose her, and it was really out of desperation that she had come to us; she didn't expect anything. As she went through various treatments, she and I would have long discussions, almost every day. She told me about the snow in Minnesota that went above your knees and how her youngest would only draw triangles, having declared a protest against other shapes. When she left after three months, she was cured. She wrote me letters. The first ones reminded me of our times in the monastery, but then her tone changed. Whereas before she had been clear to the point of crudeness, now she spoke in riddles. Finally, in her last letter, she said that she was moving, she would send word when she arrived so that I could join her. She said we would free ourselves yet."

"From what?"

I hadn't spoken in a while, and my throat felt scratchy.

"It's hard to say."

My father was looking at him strangely.

"When was that?"

"Years and years ago."

"What did she look like?"

The monk seemed surprised.

"I don't look at women as other men do."

My father held his gaze for a few more seconds before asking his next question.

"Where does B—— come in to it?"

My father has always preferred stories with consecutive narratives; he fears that tangents are taking the place of something he'd much rather know.

"My reply to that letter was sent back—her address was no

longer valid. Some months later, I began receiving little drawings of beaches. On the back of each, there was written out
'B——.' I've just assumed that that's the name of wherever
she is."

"And you think the drawings are of . . . the island?"

Even now, after moving to B——, I have trouble saying its
name aloud; there's something about the word that makes me
nervous.

"What else could they be?"

My father lit another cigarette for him.

"Would you go and join her if you knew where it was?"

"Would you?" When my father didn't say anything, the
monk smiled. "I think I would have said yes then, but it's been
so long now that I don't know how I feel anymore. Her last
letters intrigued me."

"Why did you think we would know about it?" asked my
father, echoing my thoughts.

"I always assume that when one of us knows something, so
do the rest."

My father looked at him with something like respect.

"I know what you mean."

The monk rose and raised his cross for the two of us to
unsatisfactorily caress and then left, all with an absent air, as if
once conjured in his mind's eye, B—— was a long time leaving.

"Why did you ask about the woman?"

My father avoided my eyes.

"Curiosity."

"Do you know her?"

Clearly, anything was possible when it came to my father's
acquaintances.

"I've never even been to Minnesota."

I was still turning this over when he closed the door to his bedroom, which left nothing for me to do but go to bed as well. When I woke up, all I could remember from my dreams was a beach where everyone silently stared at the water in which two people called for help, continuing to stare even after their heads had been submerged for the last time.

On the Subject of
All That We Knew About Ayale

We were certain that Ayale was no more than fifty years old, and equally positive that he was no less than thirty-five. We were sure that Ayale was from central Ethiopia, because Tadele had a half-brother who had served in the army with a former architect who had designed a house for his wife, who'd frequented the general store of a woman whose sister had a son that Tadele swore up and down was Ayale, based on eyewitness accounts and one blurry black-and-white photograph, and all of this had happened in Dire Dawa, known as Ethiopia's Europe before actual Europeans came and thought otherwise.

We knew that Ayale's real first name was Ayale, and we knew that Ayale's real last name was locked safe in his mind, away from all legal documentation, where he had deemed it wiser for it to be noted as "Abebe," the Ethiopian equivalent of

"Smith." We knew that Ayale had no middle name, but that was because none of us did. We knew that Ayale was not an only child because there had once been a sister: the barber at Egleston Square had some friends who sold *injera* out of the 7-Eleven in Jamaica Plain, who feuded with a man named Jerry, who had done her tax returns. We knew that no matter how flimsy this woman's proof of sisterhood, there was always something in these claims because if nothing else, we were all a little bit related. We didn't know her name, but by Jerry's account, she was petite with lighter skin than Ayale and a cute upturned nose that Jerry had commented on, which had made her laugh, because Jerry was a lech, but the kind that most women, including his wife, appreciated.

We knew that Ayale did not live in Dorchester, Roslindale, Roxbury, Alewife, Dudley, Chelsea, Somerville, Brookline, Brighton, Cambridge, the South End, the North End, Newton, anywhere near Mass General, Newbury Street, Copley, or West Roxbury. That being said, we didn't actually know where he lived.

We knew that he slept with many women: their husbands and boyfriends were always at the lot, complaining about their cuckolding except when he was there and they would hastily praise his newest ideas about Libyan legislation. We knew that none of these women stayed for long. We knew that Ayale did not like women who smoked outside, preferring it when they smoked in bars. This made me uncomfortable. We knew that he was partial to women who were crazy, women who were stupid, women who had issues with their fathers, women who were broken beyond compare, women who had tried to major in history at Columbia and left to have children with a gang member who was serving life in prison while his sons smoked crack in their mother's apartment, but never women who were fat, never women who were ugly, never women who loved him. This made me feel exceptional.

We knew that Ayale needed glasses but refused to buy a pair. He would take our glasses from us when the writing was too small or the view in a direction seemed too interesting to miss, no matter how many times we told him that glasses didn't work like that. We knew that Ayale had selective hearing problems, but there were medical ones, too. We knew that Ayale didn't like people who drove drunk, but he did like people who drank too much. We knew that Ayale drank gin and tonics but only in Ethiopian restaurants where they were stingy with their alcohol and there was no danger of getting drunk. We knew that he had never smoked anything but tobacco, fully supported the legalization of marijuana, and actively avoided anyone whom he knew to smoke it. We knew that Ayale appreciated chewers of *khat* as purveyors of infectious wit and wisdom, even though everyone we knew who was addicted to the stuff was a bottomless pit of nonsense and laziness.

We knew that Ayale owned a guitar. We did not know if he knew how to play it. We knew that Ayale used to go to the movies but then stopped. We knew that Ayale had a flair for interior design, picking women's shoes, and intuiting the weights of suitcases without using a bathroom scale like the rest of us. We knew that he was useless when it came to do-it-yourself projects, technology, electricity, garage doors that wouldn't go up or down, missing keys, found keys to missing locks. We knew that Ayale had a dream job in mind but that it was too late for him to obtain it. I knew that Ayale wanted his dream job to be my dream job, but it was difficult because I was slowly realizing that we did not share the same dreams, no matter how hard I tried. We knew that Ayale had achieved high levels of higher education, which was why he felt that he was a bit too good for everything around him, and we mostly all the time agreed with this.

We knew that Ayale had no regrets. I knew that Ayale officially had no regrets.

We knew that Ayale's mother had had some people killed back home, but for the right reasons. We knew that Ayale was no longer close to his mother, but we did not know if she was alive, and I knew that Ayale didn't, either.

We knew that Ayale had wanted to be a soccer player and had almost succeeded. We knew that Ayale did not like his legs because they were too skinny, but we admired their nimbleness. We knew that Ayale liked his beard, and we secretly thought he'd be better off without it.

We knew that Ayale believed in friendship and family. I knew that Ayale believed in the sacrifice inherent in those two concepts, particularly when friends or family had to sacrifice for him. We knew that he had no children. We did not know if the rumors about a previous marriage were true, but if they were, her name was Imebate, she had arrived in Boston by fleeing through Sudan, her gums were tattooed with crosses, she did not speak so much as scream, and they had parted ways when she had gone to Houston, gone Pentecostal, and never gone back.

Ayale loved cassette tapes of Motown, Alemayehu Eshete, Tilahun Gessesse, and Hirut Bekele. He kept up on music from back home, playing us the latest hits, as we marveled at his knowledge of this poor excuse for pop culture.

At some point, we all chipped in and bought him a laptop, which he used to watch every single parliamentary gathering in Addis Ababa. It got to the point where an undersecretary of a minister of agriculture couldn't sneeze without Ayale being informed of the fact, the cause, the consequences, the solutions.

I began to forget the order of the American presidents; the Johns, Williams, and Georges were displaced by tribes in the north, iron-working Jews, battles with Italy that left Eritrea out in the cold. I knew that Ayale's favorite emperor was Menelik because he was an excellent administrator, and Ayale knew that my favorite was Tewodros because he was fucking crazy, shot himself before the English could, and overall had spirit.

There were other things we thought we knew about Ayale, but they were the products of independent information gathering, espied glances, dropped hints, impatient gestures that were cut off in the middle, raised eyebrows, winks at the sky, bitten fingernails, new shirts that appeared on a Monday and had disappeared by Wednesday. We thought we understood what would make him angry and what wouldn't, but we didn't, we hadn't the first clue, actually. We thought we could give pleasure to Ayale, but it turned out that giving pleasure to Ayale was far more pleasurable for us than it was for him. We could tell when Ayale was tired, when Ayale had smelled something he didn't like, when Ayale wanted to be alone, when Ayale wanted us to stay, when Ayale wanted one of us to buy him a raincoat so that he wouldn't have to use the umbrella that one of us had already given him because we'd forgotten that Ayale didn't like umbrellas.

We knew that Ayale liked early morning waking and late afternoon to early evening napping, but we did not know where his habits came from and why he persisted in them. We did not know if he was losing time, making time, gaining time, ignoring time, forgetting time, fearing time, keeping a sharp lookout on time. We were never entirely sure if Ayale even believed in the concept of time. I sometimes thought that Ayale had created it, because it bent itself to his will in a way that it never did for anyone else I knew, especially me.

There was little that the collective knew about Ayale that I didn't also know, but the few things that they knew which I didn't, not for a long time, not consciously, are what stay with me now. I feel as though I'm carrying Ayale with me at all times, although for whom and for what reason escapes me. The weight is often unbearable, but I am terrified of what would happen if I were to let go completely. I fear that I would no longer recognize myself.

ON THE SUBJECT OF
THE VICISSITUDES OF TELEPHONIC
COMMUNICATION (I)

My father never once changed our landline number. He spoke as if this was a sustained victory against unknown forces which would be only too happy to see a shift, even of a single digit.

The first time I gave my number to another human being, in the hope that he or she would use it to call me, was when I was eleven and we had to communicate with our partners for a photosynthesis assignment. I was partnered with the repulsive Christopher Cooper, who had "behavioral problems"; he called me on Saturday night, launched into a bewildering tale about a panther (although, to be fair, I had trouble concentrating, what with my father staring at me for the whole of the one-sided conversation), and, when Monday morning rolled around, calmly passed off my work as a collective endeavor. I remained hopeful that this could be the start of a real friendship, but I quickly abandoned the notion when I heard the end of the panther story.

My most traumatic telephone experience took place in my thirteenth year, when a man with a deep voice would call to tell me what he was going to do to my body, first with his tractor and then with what he called "Einstein's Pussy-Pully System to the Stars." After a couple of weeks, he stopped calling and we were told at the monthly school assembly that there was a man targeting homes where children were known to live, harassing them with "strongly worded and inappropriate language." My depression over his disappearance was compounded with the new awareness that I was just one of many to whom he had spun his enchanting tales of simultaneous push-pull techniques.

There was no explanation for Ayale calling; I had never given him our number (he had never asked) and I had discovered that my father hated Ayale and vice versa. I didn't understand why, since as far as I knew, they hadn't seen each other since the night I came home late.

He first called after I had been visiting him for half a year, to make sure I'd gotten home. Solomon Negga, the proprietor of the store where most of us got the spices that we complained tasted nothing like home, had been found lying behind the counter, his head in a plastic bag. Ayale reassured me that he'd felt no pain.

"But how can you know?" I gasped. Solomon had always given me free bags of chips, off-brand and never spicy ranch.

"Science."

"That reminds me of someone."

"Who?"

I considered explaining about the monk.

"Never mind."

"Stay away from that area for a while."

"Are there police everywhere?"

"Apparently not." He sounded puzzled.

"How did you get my number?"

He laughed.

"Information is always there when you look in the right places."

"That doesn't explain anything."

"I'm glad you're okay. See you tomorrow."

"But—" He was gone.

"Who was that?" asked my father.

"Solomon from the store is dead," I blurted.

He looked at the ceiling for a moment.

"My mother used to say that God stopped sending plagues because He realized it would be faster to wait until we destroyed ourselves."

I didn't know what I'd expected, but it certainly wasn't this.

"Do you believe that?"

"Anything is possible in America. Isn't that why we came?"

Ayale had the habit of hanging up as soon as he felt finished with a conversation. Even if you were in mid-sentence, the phone would come crashing down, and it would be up to you to call back if what you had left to say was important, although he might beg to differ. It reminded me of how television characters never say good-bye, their telephonic conversations mere devices to advance the plot. He would trail off at the end of each exchange, repeating bye, bye, bye . . . ciao, ciao, ciao . . . right up until his click, so that you couldn't get a salutation in edgewise.

I began to expect his call upon arriving at the house, often timed so perfectly that I would still be entering when my father silently handed me the receiver. The frequency and consistency of his calls fluctuated—one week he would call every day, sometimes twice an evening when he remembered something too urgent or hysterical to let lie, while other weeks he would maybe call once if I was lucky.

After each phone conversation, my father would force me to repeat both sides of the exchange, as close to verbatim as I could manage. When I complained, he calmly explained that if I preferred, he could install another receiver in his room and listen in. I knew he wasn't bluffing and sulkily went along with his routine. After I had finished recounting, he would continue to stare and I would be aware that he was terribly frightened of me.

For a brief period, Ayale waited until he was sure that neither of us would be home in order to leave me long messages, where he'd ramble on a given subject before simply vanishing. He stopped after my father told me to tell him that it was creepy. This was the catalyst for our first Important Discussion about Ayale.

"Can I ask you a question?"

"Yeah—yes?"

"What *exactly* do you do when you go to that lot?"

"I already told you: homework. And I talk to Ayale and I help with stuff in the booth, but only if I'm done with my homework—he's very clear about that."

"What a saint."

"Why do you hate him so much?"

"Why do you like him so much?"

"You don't even know him."

"A grown man has no business spending so much time with a fifteen-year-old who isn't related to him."

"I'm almost sixteen! And at least one of the grown men I know cares about me!"

He left the apartment. When he returned with a bag of gro-

ceries and barely a glance in my direction, I became aware of the
pain in my jaw, only then unclenched: I'd been planning what
I'd do if he pulled his age-old disappearing trick. I didn't ask
what took him so long and he didn't volunteer the information.
The subject of Ayale was not brought up again that night.

Immediately following this was an entire week during which
Ayale didn't call. To say that I feared the worst would be melo-
dramatic, since I continued to see him every day at the lot and
he continued to treat me like a favored pet, but I *was* scared of
something. To add a dimension to our relationship and then
take it away with so little warning seemed cruel—I felt as
though I had been tested and found lacking. Only now does
it seem obvious that allowing one person so much power in a
two-person relationship was the first of my mistakes.

I determinedly conducted myself as though everything were
proceeding normally and, if anything, was more cheerful than
before. Meanwhile, I began to suspect Ayale and the other attendants, though of what, I couldn't say. I felt like the punch line to
a joke that everyone but me was appreciating: the smiles of the
others, which had seemed affectionate, now came off as conde-
scending, the bare minimum required by common courtesy. I
sensed that Ayale was more distracted than usual—or did he
want me to think this so that I would leave him be?

Maintaining this forced equanimity proved too much for my
system—I developed the flu, then a thick cough, and then bron-
chitis, immediately after midterms. I stayed in bed until May of
that year, and when I finally recovered, was three inches taller,
fifteen pounds lighter, and felt like I'd been magicked into a
completely different person.

While I was bedridden, Ayale called and stopped by the
house almost unceasingly. In my initial half-consciousness, it
was like watching an unending film reel, composed of Ayale

coming, Ayale going, Ayale speaking words I didn't hear. My father soon stopped allowing him into my room, supposedly because his visits caused the fever to skyrocket—no one was more detrimental to my health, he liked to say. I still think that he used my sickness to take back from Ayale what he perceived as his power. I know that Ayale never forgave him for barring him entrance, and there was a new viciousness on the rare occasions when he spoke of my father.

The first day I was well enough to attend school and visit the lot (my father and I had had another quarrel that morning), each attendant hugged and kissed me, and Ayale himself ushered me into the booth, where I sat in the chair that was usually reserved for him. I wondered if I had imagined the coldness of before, if perhaps my addled mind had conjured up those demons, like the high-strung male protagonists in Dostoevsky's novels, prone to unending maladies that drive them to commit terrible deeds and envision the most monstrous of apparitions. I almost convinced myself that my body and I were the root causes of any darkness shed upon Ayale; I almost believed that he wasn't the instigator of all the small doubts and corrosions that were taking their toll.

But this is foreshadowing, a cheap, if sometimes entertaining, trick. At that point, I was just happy to be alive in a world where Ayale existed. It wouldn't have occurred to me to be happy without him; I had nearly forgotten what that was like.

During my convalescence, I'd confronted him about the cessation of calls. He seemed surprised that I'd noticed, which might have been because it had had so little impact on him. Perhaps very different moments served as landmarks or landmines in our lives.

"I was busy."

His face gave away nothing, except maybe boredom with this line of thought.

"Of course you were."

"What are you trying to say?"

"Nothing! Just that that was what I thought."

"Were you waiting for me to call?"

"No."

"Was there something you wanted to say to me?"

"Absolutely not."

He shook his head.

"You women are all the same sometimes."

He refused to elaborate, and the statement both pleased and irritated me.

Without another word on the subject, Ayale and I took our own measures to make the telephone a secret tool in our employ. He stopped calling during the times when my father was likely to be awake, and I stayed up later, answering the phone on the first ring, listening, and then soundlessly replacing the receiver. If my father happened to be there, I would tell him it was a wrong number and watch one of the many shows that we had formed the collective habit of watching, in order to avoid his gaze. The messages were never long, usually instructions as to where we were meeting for a South Street Diner expedition, reminders to clarify the hypothesis for my Cold War paper, information about the valet parking attendant who exploded in a stolen Lexus, warnings that it was likely to snow the next day. What I saw was being remolded into what Ayale wanted me to see, a state that I defined as "adulthood" in my sixteenth year.

On the Subject of South Street Diner

Ayale said their corned beef was the best in town, and I was inclined to agree. The only twenty-four-hour eating establishment in Boston, South Street Diner's fluorescent green, pink, and white sign features a white coffee mug with the name of the café and the fact that it's open twenty-four hours in flashing letters, so that any late-night driver can see it and decide that a hot mug and a BLT might be just the thing to make it all fine again.

South Street Diner claims to be at the heart of Boston's late-night scene, which could be true if Boston *had* a late-night scene. Instead, South Street Diner is a compilation album of blue-collar workers, insomniacs, and Emerson students, the last of which are the scourge of the earth, don't let anyone tell you different.

Ayale and I didn't fall into any of these categories. Our periodic descents into the trailer-like décor began, according to my journal, two weeks after I recovered from the sickness that ushered me back into the parking lot fold. That Saturday, at around two A.M., our phone rang and I raced to answer it before my father woke up. Minutes later, a car honked, I tiptoed out with shoes in hand, and a freshly scrubbed Ayale nodded at me. This became a frequent-enough occurrence that it soon felt like ritual.

We hightailed it to Kneeland Street, taking the way that slid us past the lot. Things were going to change, according to Ayale.

"I'm only staying at the lot until I save up enough money," he said, hands at the ten and two positions on the steering wheel. Fear of the police had transformed him into a stupendous driver.

"What will you do with the money?"

"I'll go back home."

"And then?"

"Consulting, most probably."

"The prime minister's right-hand man?"

I said these words without thinking. I had never been to Ethiopia, and didn't much care that I hadn't; I just assumed it would happen one day. Whenever a teacher first heard my name and feigned curiosity as to its origins, starting or ending with an insincere "It's so pretty!" I wanted to protest, I'm American! What's an Ethiopia? How does one come to be there? How does one come to leave it to go to an America? But in truth, I was only almost American, so I gave my explanations and nothing else of myself until the bell rang.

"Addis Ababa may not be a factor anymore," Ayale said mysteriously.

"How do you mean?"

"Things change."

"For the better, I hope."

"Always."

He gently pulled my hair as we slid into an empty space near the restaurant. I chose a table far enough away from both the door and the bathroom, while Ayale ordered two corned beef sandwiches, with extra fries for him and extra onions for me. He brought one of the napkin dispensers by the cash register back to our table because Ethiopians never understand that the napkins aren't going anywhere; each food item requires a year's supply, with a few concealed on one's person upon departure. Ayale had already started eating by the time I returned from washing my hands. I watched as he drenched his fries with the hot sauce that no one but us ever used.

"Think you used enough dynamite there, Butch?"

"What a stupid movie."

"Who is this guy?" I asked the restaurant at large.

"That's not even the line."

"One must improvise in times of trouble."

"I'm troubled by your obsession with Robert Redford."

"Are you referring to my devotion to a cinematic icon? A legend?"

"What about Denzel Washington? Robert De Niro?"

"This isn't *Highlander*. There can be more than one."

"Just eat."

He let me chew for a few minutes before he stole more of my fries.

"How's school?"

"Fine."

"Lot of work?"

"It's okay."

"How's math going?"

"I'm trying."

"Ouch."

I followed his hand as it poked around the greasy sandwich wrappers, hoping to unearth uneaten scraps, and as his fingers grazed the burnt end of a fry, I swiftly slam-dunked it into my mouth. I collapsed into shrieks as people turned and he shook his head.

"You can't count *and* you're heartless. Good luck getting married."

I laughed harder. Our few neighbors were smiling as they turned back to their conversations, as if whatever they'd thought had been proven wrong. I didn't let my mind linger on their reactions as Ayale pretended to slap me with a napkin.

"Are you finished?"

I nodded but then dissolved again. He chuckled.

"I'm going to get a coffee. Let me know when you're done—I want to ask you something."

He returned with a mug in one hand and another napkin dispenser in the other. I knew the latter was to make me laugh, so I did.

"What did you want to ask me?"

"How much is your allowance?"

I named the pitiful sum. He looked astonished.

"Per day or per week?"

It was my turn to look astonished.

"Per week."

"Would you be interested in making a little extra?"

"I'm always interested in making a little extra."

"That's the most American thing you've ever said."

I wasn't in the mood for jokes anymore.

"What are we talking about here?"

"I need you to drop some things off for me, every week."

"I can't be home late."

"When you get to the lot, your deliveries will be ready. You'll go at the time I tell you, you'll leave your things in the booth, you'll come back, you'll do your homework. An hour or less."

"Could I do it before school?"

"Not possible."

"Can I ask you another question?"

"Of course. How else will you learn?"

"What will I be delivering?"

"Relatives in Ethiopia get confused with addresses, which means things get lost in the mail. I thought the parking lot could be a kind of depot for Boston: everyone sends their packages there, and we make sure everything goes to the right place."

"That's a pretty good idea."

"It means the world to me that you approve. Will you do it or not?"

His tone alarmed me, but he was still smiling, so I let it go.

"Yes."

His voice lost its edge with the next question.

"Don't you want to know how much you'll make?"

I sensed that if I didn't get excited about the money, the blade in his voice would return.

"How much?"

"Thirty bucks per delivery." He laughed at my expression. "We'll start on Friday. Good?"

"Great," I squeaked.

He gave me a closer look.

"You need to start sleeping more."

"I try."

"You need to eat more."

"Stop eating my food then."

"The key is to take naps. Look at me: I don't exercise, I don't watch what I eat, I smoke, and I'm never sick. Why? A strict regimen of napping. Every day. Even if it's only for a half hour, I close my eyes, I go away, and when I come back, I feel *fresh*."

For Ayale, feeling fresh was the highest degree of health and happiness that anyone could hope to achieve.

"Naps make me feel worse."

"You're not letting yourself get used to them. You need to create a schedule of sleep and stick to it."

"How?"

"You find a time when you're never busy and you take a nap then, for however long you want. You keep taking a nap at that exact time, for that exact same *amount* of time, every day. Soon, your body will get tired on its own and it'll teach itself to feel fresh afterward."

Ayale was a slave to no one, not even his own body. I could picture him as a kid, riding a zebra out the door past curfew, unfazed by his mother's screams. It wasn't power I wanted, just impunity: I didn't care about riding a zebra, I only wanted to be sure that no consequences would follow, no zebra tax would be imposed. If Ayale ever got caught, he would just explain the inherent rationale of what he was doing, the authorities would admit their stupidity, and he would emerge victorious.

I recognize that some might meet Ayale and not get swept up in his spell, might find him unkempt and horrible, especially in light of what happened later, but he remains the greatest man I'll ever know, and unlike some, I'm not ashamed to say it. Sometimes, however, the best people are the worst for us to love; I'm learning to accept that.

"It seems like a lot of work."

"Nothing's more important than your health."

I felt drunk as we drove back, without knowing what that was. Deliveries could lead to greater responsibilities, could lead to trust, could lead to friendship, could turn into family. And once you're *really* family, you can never be kicked out. You'll never be alone.

"Does Solomon's family know what happened?" I suddenly asked, talk of Ethiopian relatives having brought to mind the rumors swapped by mainstays of the lot.

He nodded.

"His siblings left to see their parents."

"Is it true that he stole money from the store?"

Ayale gave me a look.

"I think what's true and what's not when it comes to the dead is none of our business."

Within weeks, I'd forgotten about Solomon.

My father began to demand that I hand over my keys after getting home. I flirted with the idea of asking Ayale if I could live with him, but the potential humiliation and hurt of him saying no was too nauseating to consider. Instead, Ayale had one of the attendants make multiple copies of my keys, so that he'd always have a spare. My father only managed to keep me from the diner once, and I spent the day excessively moping and being hungry, no matter how many spaghetti products were shoved into my face. If my father learned that I had found a way around his rules, he never mentioned it. He started shutting himself up in his room, materializing only to use the bathroom or go to work. Days would go by when we wouldn't see each other. Only once did he ask if I had anything to tell him, and I replied no. I imagine now that during those weeks of silence, he was steeling himself to watch as I betrayed him again and again and again. Perhaps his staying put was penance for not doing so before.

Sometimes, when we were lucky, Ayale and I would see the sun rise on our way home from the diner. However, what with air pollution and the sun growing reluctant to rise over this rapidly spreading wasteland of fitness centers, condos, and an ever-dwindling Chinatown, it was a rare thing.

On the Subject of
How I Came to Genuinely Suspect

Three months later, I'd made eighteen deliveries and zero friends. Ayale paid promptly and often tipped, and while I enjoyed the newfound affluence, I had nowhere to spend my money, and I sometimes felt like the servers and busboys he tipped extravagantly, even in fast food places, where they often forgot to thank him as they furtively slipped his twenties into their pockets, a blatant breach of the no-gratuities rule. I knew I should be grateful for his money and time, but the effort made me irritable with everyone else; suddenly, there was no more room with the unpopular Asian girls. I took to eating lunch in the third-floor bathroom, vacant since Kelly Dylan's suicide, fourth stall down.

It was around this time that Fiker arrived, on the heels of another murder. A full-page article provided the details. Name:

Kebede, although everyone (Americans) called him Kebs; employed at the Ukrainian Orthodox church; killed while cleaning candles (ever industrious); no children, no wife; whereabouts when he wasn't fulfilling his liturgical duties unknown. The journalist described him as reserved, although how he'd reached this conclusion about someone no one seemed to have spoken to was one of the many tricks the press hid up its black-and-white sleeve.

Older Ethiopians recalled there being a scandal in his past, involving war, Italy, a dead sister, but it was the sweet-and-sour irony of blood-soaked hands working in tandem with the sacraments that proved irresistible: everyone had *just* the right proverb or verse to explain, define, or justify. By the time of his death, Kebs was nearly a deacon, fifty-seven, and his passport hadn't been renewed in twenty years. The news story confirmed that it was murder, with all other details pending. They continued to pend by the time I left.

Days later, I was dragging myself to the lot, teetering under the combined weight of textbooks, notebooks, and graded binders. It was about to rain, a constant state of affairs. I was almost level with the first cars when I saw Ayale, nodding his head at an enormous man. I had never seen Ayale allow someone else to speak for this long without interrupting; he seemed rapt. I didn't like it. I ran back in the direction from which I'd come, took a breath at the corner, tired myself out with internal debate, decided the only way out is forward, and sauntered toward the lot, looking at the sky, the ground, the trees, anything but my intended destination. Ayale was sitting inside the booth, smoking a cigarette, reading one of his daily papers. He smiled at my arrival, but I was too busy looking for the giant to reciprocate.

"Where is he?"

"Who?"

"The man you were talking to."

Ayale closed his eyes.

"Were you spying on me?"

"No! I forgot something, over there"—I gestured in the vague direction of behind—"and when I came back, he was gone."

He opened his eyes.

"Don't you have homework?"

I retreated to his car, doors open because the windows no longer worked. From then on, I kept my mouth shut and my eyes open. In the next few weeks, I noted how the kinds of manila envelopes I'd seen on my first day were a daily presence in the booth. When Ayale left to buy cigarettes or coffee, the packages were stuffed into his pockets or, if too bulky, entrusted to an attendant, who couldn't leave his side. They looked nothing like my neatly wrapped deliveries, and were immediately passed to others, the receiver of the parcel acting as if he and Ayale had bumped into each other, victims of clumsiness or narrow streets. These recipients were sometimes wearing Boston Police Department uniforms, were sometimes a woman named Elsie (whom I'd later find out was Fiker's wife), Ayale's boss Lentil, or the Sudanese security guard across the street whose name was Thomas and whose front teeth were missing.

I found Ayale increasingly evasive. He couldn't remember how he had decided to work there, he wasn't sure if they received overtime, he wavered on how he reconciled his profound fear of the police with his constant cooperation, he didn't want to discuss how so few customers were turned away, he pled the fifth on his feelings toward female attendants, he had no memory of speaking with a large man who had now vanished. Our conversations became cat-and-mouse chases of inquisition and avoidance, casual inquiries into money, cars, Thomas deftly turned aside by generalities and expressions of fatigue.

Around the same time, my father and I started getting used to each other and I joined a summer theater company, where I learned stage fighting. That kept me going until September.

That fall, Ayale taught me how to smoke with his Winstons. The first lesson was inhaling, and took up the better part of a week. The second lesson was style. My fingers immediately fell into a placement unintentionally copied from my father; I lacked the nerve to buy a cigarette holder and smoke like Bette Davis. I've always loved the smell of cigarette smoke, although I'd thought I would never smoke myself; I was too afraid of cancer, aging, losing my teeth, losing my eyesight, losing my sex drive, losing my sex appeal, whenever I managed to find it. Nonetheless, when Ayale offered me that first cigarette, I accepted without question.

Later, he would wish that he'd spared me a habit that prevented him from visiting Ethiopia, since spending eighteen airborne hours smokeless was unthinkable. Ayale came to see smoking as his personal curse, while simultaneously believing that his life had only begun on the day of his first puff. This, he told me while we traded bites of ice cream, was a little bit like a catch-22. I told him that I'd read the book, and he said, Reading a book is one thing, seeing events as they unfold is totally different. I tried to hide just how much I loved smoking.

We were sharing the last of a pack, mere weeks into eleventh grade, when I decided to confront him.

"What's going on?"

"Many things."

"Who was that man?"

He sighed.

"Everything is going to be all right."

I tried a different tack.

"You would tell me if something was going on?"

"I would tell you if something was going on."

"Don't just repeat what I say, tell me like it's something that you genuinely believe."

What I left unspoken was just how desperately I needed to believe it as well.

"*I* would *tell* you if *something* was *going on.*"

"You sound like a bad actor."

"You've become a bit unbearable since that theater thing."

"You didn't come to any of the shows."

"I didn't have time."

"You don't work on the weekends."

"I don't like American theater. It's too American."

"But I was in it. It doesn't matter what you think in theory when there's someone important to you who's involved. You support them always."

"And that applies to everything?"

"Please, don't turn this into a grand, overarching statement about the Ethiopian political atmosphere, and what this means I think about it, and how what I think about it is precisely the wrong thing to think about it, or shows that I'm not exercising my mental capacities in the way that I'm capable of. Please. Just answer the question you know I'm asking."

I loved Ayale more than anyone, but he was beginning to exhaust me.

"You say that like it's something I would actually do."

I laughed in spite of my irritation.

"Look, if I support you no matter what, would you do the same for me?"

Ayale's sincerity was heartbreaking on the rare occasions when he displayed it, perhaps only because it *was* so rare.

"Absolutely."

Ayale thoughtfully opened a new pack. My father didn't know I smoked. He finally spoke.

"His name is Fiker, and I will tell you whenever and if ever there is anything to tell. That's the rule for both of us."

We shook hands, kissed two times on the cheeks, and then I walked to the T because Ayale had a few stops to make before he went home. He gave me twenty dollars for transportation because he didn't trust my T pass. I tried to be happy about it.

On the Subject of Some Teachers I Once Had

With no answers forthcoming and three free periods to fill, I threw myself into photography, which our high school would offer for two years before concluding that the accumulating visual evidence of the world around us was wreaking irreversible emotional harm and inciting the increasing cases of depression. The real artists took it the first year because their parents were ex-hippies who had dabbled in art before settling down to be bank directors, doctors, and small business owners. The second year was when everyone else took it, after discovering that nothing set a person apart more than a camera around their neck, like a noose. I was one of the second-year kids. I was always one of the second-year kids.

The photography teacher's name was Andrew Phillips, but everyone called him Philly. Philly wore floral dress shirts and got away with it. No one called him a fag, even out of his hearing. He had half a goatee, and I wondered if something had happened to him, because it didn't occur to me that someone might do that intentionally. Philly was the palest man I had ever seen. His skin was shiny without being oily: he glowed. Philly was so tall that his head regularly hit the ceiling, his hair was floppy chestnut, and he spoke like a clever quote book, with the benefit (or grace) of making it seem as though these statements came to him on the spur of the moment, the way others conjured up articles and conjunctions. It was how I imagined Mark Twain or Oscar Wilde to have spoken. I used to write down what people said if I found it funny, and I now see that if anyone overused the word "proverbial," it was Philly.

"Ah yes, the proverbial red herring!" he would boom out when we showed him black and whites of peace rallies and bankrupt supermarkets. This was classic Philly: nonsensical, yet hilarious.

I had no knack for photography. I couldn't open the canisters, my exposures were wildly off because I didn't understand how and when to change them, and my subjects were blurry. Nonetheless, I had, by far, the most ambitious ideas. Philly once congratulated me on my vision when he and I were the last ones in the darkroom, him patiently wresting open the canisters that I had already mangled with my efforts. I had done a series featuring a pair of headless Barbies who engaged in a lovers' quarrel that ended with Malibu Barbie giving Pocahontas Barbie her right arm as a token of her devotion. The images were muddy and my captions were illegible, but Philly laughed harder than anyone during my presentation and gave me an A for the semester.

I began spending Tuesday and Thursday evenings in the studio, on the pretext of developing pictures. I told Ayale and my father that I was getting physics tutoring. Philly would tell me stories of growing up in Vermont and being Indian-burned by someone you loved. I didn't love Philly, but I wanted his unconditional approval and undivided attention. Loving someone and wanting love from someone are usually diametrically opposed emotions, and it took me a long time to understand that, long past the point when Philly left and I had to look elsewhere.

My English teacher taught in the basement and began each class with detailed descriptions of how the air around us was probably giving us stage I lung cancer. We called him Mr. C, and his dark stubble perfectly suited his weathered face and his plaid suspenders. He was the first person to fail me. The test was on *Black Boy*, and I cornered him as soon as class ended, ignoring the kids who had to climb over my oversized backpack.

"What is this?" I spat out.

"It's the grade you deserved." He looked amused.

"I read that book three times."

"It shows."

"I should have aced this test."

"And yet you didn't."

"*Why?*"

Mr. C grinned as he fiddled with the silver bracelet that soothed his arthritis.

"What you did only works on multiple-choice tests and asshole teachers who don't know how to teach. This was an essay test. I wanted your thoughts. You didn't give me your thoughts. You recited the book back to me. That's not learning. That's being a trained poodle, and so I gave you the grade I would give to a trained poodle."

"You must be joking."

He guided me toward the door.

"I rarely joke in public. Take a goddamn aspirin and calm down. It's one test, not the rest of your life."

I began to request extra oral book reports with him. When he asked why, I would point to the failed test and explain that I needed to raise my average. In the middle of the last one I wrangled out of him, he closed the book before I'd finished.

"I'm not done."

"You're never done."

"No seriously, there's just one more thing that I want to say, and then I'll be done."

"I have to tell you something."

"Was I wrong?"

"I'm not going to be your father."

"That's ridiculous."

"I am not here to be a substitute for something you don't have."

At our last conference, he asked me what I was planning on doing in college. I told him that I didn't know and he smiled, for the first time seeming almost proud of me.

"That's the best response."

"That's idiotic," Ayale told me afterward. "Everyone needs to know what they want to do."

"What if you genuinely don't know?"

"You're just not trying hard enough."

"Questioning is the most important step."

"Bullshit."

He was closing up the booth as he spoke, and as I watched his familiar movements, I was surprised to feel a kind of fatigue. I was never good enough for him, and he was never what I wanted him to be, no matter how hard I strained to make him so. I didn't notice how closely Ayale was scrutinizing me until he spoke again.

"You're better than that."

"Excuse me?"

I was afraid he'd read my thoughts. He often did.

"You're better than the garbage that privileged white people can afford to tell you because they have no investment in you. They don't know that if you or I were to run around, talking about how we're too busy feeling and finding ourselves to look for a real job, we'd be considered jokes, at best. When he and his friends tried it, they were congratulated for being a youth revolution. This isn't our country. We can't play the games the natives play."

"I was born here."

"It doesn't matter. I'm sorry, but it's true."

He hesitated before leaning close to my ear.

"Just you wait: our people were meant for greater things. I'll get you there. I'll get you there even if I die doing it."

Mr. C's dismissal was school-wide knowledge the next day. I realized that Ayale didn't have to read my mind anymore, since he was too busy seeing the future and making those who angered him pay heavily in it. He was winning both the battle and the war, although only now did I see that there was a struggle. That night, I dreamt of a God with Ayale's face.

On the Subject of the Disciples

No one remembered when or how, but in what seemed like too little time to judge anyone's trustworthiness, Fiker and Ayale had become inseparable. It was obvious that they'd known each other for years, although nothing about this shared past was ever divulged. Fiker was the largest human I'd ever seen; he ate nothing until evening and then didn't stop consuming food until he passed out from whiskey. Ayale disapproved but always caved into indulgent laughter as Fiker recounted the previous night's misadventures: how he'd kissed a woman who wasn't his wife, had fallen down the stairs of a house that wasn't his own, proved yet again that Ayale held fast to a moral high ground that Fiker hadn't even suspected could exist. Nonetheless, Ayale recognized the man's intellectual acuity, on par

with his own, if not a bit sharper in some areas, and their close-
ness deepened at the same rate as their mutual distrust.

Along with Fiker came Elsie, whose visits to the lot would
end with her husband shoving her off the premises, her beating
him with whatever came to hand first, the rest of us pretending we'd temporarily lost sight and hearing, and Ayale never
intervening. Everyone knew she was the only reason Fiker
wasn't dead, although it sometimes felt like she might kill him
herself. It was Elsie who'd rescued her husband from wherever he was before Boston—location and circumstances never
defined or requested—and it was Elsie who'd wheedled a job out
of Ayale. No matter how many times Fiker offended, attacked,
stumbled, she stayed by his side, radiant, persuading, laughing, as
one by one, the women, the charges, the accusations evapo-
rated. We knew nothing about what she did as pastime or career
but understood that while you might get a broken leg from Fiker,
we were never going to see you again once Elsie was through.
She acted as though I wasn't present, which only added to
her appeal: I would have given anything to look and behave
like her.

I'd become all eyes and few words since Fiker's arrival. It
took only our introduction for me to grasp how he loved to
mock me, how delicious he found my envy.

"Do you know what 'Fiker' means?"

Such a simple question was insulting.

"Love."

"Look at you! Learning words, remembering words, saying
words . . . you've trained her well."

Ayale didn't glance up from his newspaper.

"She came to me like that."

I didn't appreciate being described as trained, like I was a
dog. I aimed for a cutting tone.

"And what do you do?"

"I observe."

"And then what?"

"I act upon what I've seen."

"In what way?"

"In whatever way seems appropriate."

"What are you observing now?"

Fiker smiled. Despite his constant exhibition of unfettered joy, his smiles and laughs never touched his eyes; every indication of elation got cut off at seemingly predetermined moments. This was his slow special, merely raising his lips to expose his brown teeth, nearly the same shade as his caked skin.

"You're still a little girl. You may think you're ready for more, but I'd keep that to yourself. Once word gets out, it's hard to shove it back in."

His eyes lingered on me before abruptly turning. I felt filthy for the rest of the day.

Having Fiker at the lot put the other attendants and hangers-on in stark relief. The four that had shadowed Ayale at our first meeting were neither the most nor the least important: all of them were interchangeable. They looked the same, talked the same, smoked the same, worshipped Ayale the same. They followed their leader with a passion rarely displayed in other areas of their depressed lives. They were easily identifiable by their words and actions, which mirrored those of their guide: they had been divested of themselves, with nothing of their individualities remaining. They were drenched in Ayale.

He hadn't meant to create them. He simply spoke to them as he had to others before, looking directly into their eyes, giving utterance to what he believed to be right, unflinching, beautiful. It's nearly impossible to foresee whether one will become an icon for others, a standard at the forefront of a war one did not

mean to create. There are those cocky enough to gather follow-
ers (see: Jesus Christ), although usually those with the most
ardent devotees didn't initially seek them out (see: Robert Redford). Universal, however, is the element of flattery created by
such a willing following, one that all but the strongest would
find difficult to resist. Ayale was perhaps the least capable.

At the time of Fiker's introduction, the disciples were growing too numerous and spread out to be accurately cataloged.
Ayale had divided them into categories: those in positions to
carry out favors with key people, those with banter, those willing to run errands. The women moved easily between "disciple"
and "lover," often multiple times, until Ayale or they tired of the
game. The group to which a disciple belonged was made clear
by the manner in which Ayale greeted the individual, although
one had to hover on the outskirts and retain enough interest to
notice these minute variations, I being the only person who did.

There was something unnerving about coming upon one
of the disciples without Ayale there to offset the sting. I was at
the cinema in Randolph when I recognized a new recruit to the
parking scene, the first to arrive from his Welo village, and the
first Ethiopian I'd met who'd actually seen the famine, insofar
as these things are visible. We greeted each other as we'd been
taught to as children, and then found we had nothing more
to say.

"Did you read the latest about the hurricane?" he finally
asked.

"I think so."

"Isn't it horrible?"

"Yes."

"Can you believe they're letting that shipping magnate build
his condo on the graves of those dead black kids? I almost threw
up, I was so furious."

I cautiously drew back.

"Shipping magnate?"

"Of course!"

The businessman in question, Sheldon Graves, was a point of outrage for Ayale as well and, as far as I knew, had yet to appear in a single English-language news outlet. Ayale claimed to have heard about him from an insider in the life-jacket business.

"I didn't hear about that."

The man seemed scandalized.

"It's everywhere!"

"Where *exactly* did you see this?"

I wondered if Ayale had so completely penetrated his psyche that he had ceased to associate him with how or what he learned.

"I don't need to remember where I read every little thing."

"I was just curious."

"It's a shame how little your generation cares about current events."

He raised a hand, a signal of farewell and dismissal, an exact imitation of the gesture I'd seen a million times before, always with the same hand, often with a Winston clutched between its first two fingers. It was as though Ayale moved within him, putting on this guise before taking up residence in another host.

With Fiker's arrival, Ayale appeared unsure of how best to use his ideological army, surprising since he was quite talented at espying the ways in which others could advance his goals. One day, I didn't see his car, and when I inquired, he smiled.

"I found a better way of transporting myself."

"Public transportation?"

The last time that Ayale remembered using a bus, it was to go to a used car dealership after winning six hundred dollars with Mega Millions.

"That's one way of putting it." He couldn't stop laughing. "It's public because it's available to the public . . ."

He splintered into hapless hilarity. My incomprehension only made it funnier, and so I patiently waited until he had tired himself out.

"Well?"

He only laughed again, moving toward a woman who was looking doubtfully at the rates.

I was impatient to see how Ayale would take himself homeward. He prolonged the torture by scrutinizing the sky and sighing at the uncertainty of the weather. He wondered aloud at those who depended on bicycles. He apologized profusely for not bringing his car to take me home, and he verified that I had my T pass. By the end, I was laughing, too. Five P.M. arrived, as it always does. While he locked up the booth, a taxi pulled up to the curb. Ayale raised a hand in greeting and, with the other, steered me toward its doors. The driver lowered the front passenger-side window and peered out. He looked furious.

"Can you please just get in? Please?"

"We're making two stops tonight."

"You must be joking, man! Do you realize I'm still on duty? Huh? That means I'm *working*, okay? I could get *fired* if they find out, *okay?*"

"One more stop won't make a difference."

"Actually, it's super easy to get home from here—"

"Don't be ridiculous—get inside."

"No, seriously, I'd rather take the train. I have some stuff to buy anyway."

"Then we'll take you there, too."

"No, we will *not*. Look, *yene konjo*, you'll get home faster by train, I promise."

"Right, so I'll just—"

"Are you refusing to help me?" Ayale sounded incredulous.
The man glared but was the first to look away.

"I'll take you wherever you want," he finally muttered.

"Thank you. If we hadn't wasted all this time arguing, you'd be halfway done by now."

I climbed in after him and we drove to my apartment, Ayale smoking contentedly while we raced past late night lights and people. I thanked the man upon our arrival, and when he said nothing, Ayale tapped him on the shoulder, and he grunted. Ayale winked at me.

I heard the story the following week. Our sullen cabbie was the brother of a Stuart Street attendant, a longtime Ayale acolyte. Ayale had paid for their mother's blood transfusion, and if the attendant had respected him before, there was now no one in the universe who could match his magnificence. All offers to pay the sum back were refused. One morning, Ayale arrived at the lot only to find the man prostrate before him on the ground, begging him to name anything that could serve as a meager token of his gratitude. Ayale was his true brother, not like the other vultures who passed as kinsfolk in this land of coyotes. Ayale responded that he only hoped the transfusion would take. The man wept harder.

It was then that Ayale remembered to ask after his brother: how fared the taxi business these days? Fine, sighed the man, made wretched by his debt. How lucky he was, continued Ayale, what fun, speeding around the city, meeting new people at all hours of the night, while he was saddled with a barely running sedan. The man put two and two together and noted that his brother often kept the taxi later than he should for his own joyrides; would Ayale be in need of some chauffeuring? And so it was that the one gained a driver, and the other relief from his guilt.

The truly loyal were the smallest in number. There were many fools who parroted Ayale's words to whomever would listen, but the ones who really believed were chained to him for eternity, doomed (blessed?) to be destroyed at the same moment his number came up. However, they were also the real beneficiaries of his generosity, receiving new cars, round-trip tickets to Ethiopia, promotions, apartments, medical treatment, extended time with dying parents, all paid from the depths of Ayale's capacious pockets. No matter how angry they might become, no matter how suspicious their families and friends (who soon disappeared, since being Ayale's man was a full-time job), there was simply no way to pay everything back. Even if there had been, Ethiopian insistence on infinite misery requires that the recipient of any favor, no matter how basic, be forever indebted to the giver of that favor. It's in an attempt to restore these men's dignity that I call them disciples instead of indentured servants; perhaps it's even a bestowal of holy order.

With the grafting of Fiker onto the tree of Ayale, the disciples grew confused: to whom did they now pledge themselves? Ayale had initially won preeminence through seniority, his having been there first and created them more than enough to ensure his omnipotence. Gradually, though, it became apparent that Ayale and Fiker, if not different sides of the same coin, knew that the coin existed and that it was a pretty important one, and the disciples grew unsure about whether Ayale remained supreme. Perhaps he and Fiker were engaged in a silent struggle as the latter mutinied against the former; perhaps they were brothers who must live as one in order to survive. After a month of befuddled imbalance, it was tacitly decided that Ayale was king, Fiker was first mate, and everyone had to stay on their toes: there was no telling when whatever was being kept at bay to sustain this relationship would be unleashed.

The disciples confronted parking lot procedure with the precision of a well-trained army; if the attendants were the cavalry, they were the infantry. Ayale was careful about which of his ideas he allowed to thrive among them. His ultimate design was to create a human fleet in his own image, and he and Fiker fantasized about this high-quality citizenry, a people intelligent enough to accept.

Discipledom was a thankless assignment, although that was hardly Ayale's fault; it's inherent to the gig. A casual stroll through the Bible confirms it. The disciples of Jesus were forced to abandon (at minimum): careers, incomes, the respect of others, fornication for pleasure, families, clean clothing, regular meals, self-esteem.

Before I left Boston, it was widely believed that most of the disciples were in hiding in western Massachusetts. A few drifted back into their former lives with neither a murmur nor a cry, held always at arm's length by the rest of our people. I still don't know how I feel about them, but no one can deny that they loved Ayale with an ardor that elevated them when most everything else in their lives tried to thrust them back.

ON THE SUBJECT OF THE BASEMENT COVENANT

Just as I was learning to stand Fiker's unsettling presence, my father started going away on the weekends. My father is a man of habit, most of his patterns locked firmly in place since childhood. Any potential new tendency, foodstuff, or pair of pants is deliberated over for weeks, during which time he remains entrenched in the kind of soul-searching that has broken stronger men. It's nearly impossible to ascertain when he's in the middle of one of these reflection sessions or just being his workaday self, since the usual signs of pensiveness—excessive silence, furrowed brow, vigorous smoking, solitary walks—are already principal aspects of his persona.

It was a Thursday when he made his intentions known, a small duffel bag already packed in preparation for the voyage, which he would embark upon the next day, directly after work. His destination would wait for no man.

"Where are you going?"

"Visiting."

"A person?"

For as long as I'd known him, he'd never mentioned any friends or family members, except for one or two brunch references to unknown or possibly fictitious people in Addis, most of whom had breathed their last. My father didn't attend funerals for the same reason that he didn't eat fruit in the car: principle.

"When are you coming back?"

"Sunday night."

"Why are you going?"

"I just have to straighten out a few things. I'll leave you some money." He sounded lost.

"Is everything okay?"

He began to play with the mugs on the counter.

"I'm not doing much good here, am I?"

He smiled with his mouth closed; it looked painful.

"I'm not sure what you mean."

My eyes were trying to locate a view that didn't include him.

"I mean, you'll do exactly what you want and I won't have any way of preventing that or of helping you, because, it turns out, I'm incapable of all this." He gestured vaguely at the kitchen cupboards. "I'm an incapable person."

When I didn't respond, he sighed and went to the bathroom. I fiddled with my shirt buttons, then made myself stop; I'd already disabled too many items with my nervous habit. When he came back out—I was always surprised by how little time he took, almost as if he only went to cover up the fact that he didn't have a bladder—he stood close to my chair, his hands hovering above mine, in what I believe was an attempt to hold them.

"I'm sorry for what I said."

"What?"

"You didn't need to hear that. Maybe it's good that I'm going away for a while—we can both take a break, think about what's bothering us."

"Nothing's bothering me."

"That makes one of us," he snapped. He closed his eyes. "I'm sorry."

This was my first glimpse into the constant guilt that plagued my father. He appreciated love, he wanted to do right by others, but he also wanted to be left the fuck alone, and that desire seemed so alien to everyone else around him that he was certain he was in the wrong. Even retreating was a minefield, his seclusion ruined by his sadness at deriving no comfort from the kinds of relationships that fueled everyone else. My father simply asks that those he loves let him be.

"Are you sure nothing is bothering you," he tried again. "I mean, a lot of this isn't normal."

"What isn't normal?"

"Our lives, this whole Ayale thing—"

"What *Ayale thing*?"

"The man is older than I am, and yet you two hang out like buddies. If you need friends, they should be of your own age."

Typical, how he addressed the idea of having friends as a nasty compulsion in which only some, like me, would even think to indulge.

"I'm happy with things the way they are."

"I just can't believe that."

"You're going to be late."

"For what?"

"Sleeping. Good night. And you don't have to take your keys—I mean, if you forget them, I'll be here on Sunday, I won't fall asleep."

I babbled in order to ward off the specter of mutual revelation he kept shoving into our midst.

"One more thing."

I turned slowly from the entrance to my room. It was like he'd swallowed some sort of truth serum, a laxative for the mouth. It was horrible.

"Now that we're on the subject"—which we weren't really; thinking about something that the other person has neither mentioned nor heard you think about is not at all the same as being on the subject of that something—"I've been meaning to ask you if you have any questions . . . about your mother. Or, maybe, questions about your mother and me? I wasn't sure if you'd, well, if you'd like to talk about the situation? Because maybe you're curious, perfectly natural to be curious, and you didn't know how to bring it up before?"

I felt like I was going to vomit. No amount of insistence on his part was going to transform us into that TV-movie family where having only one parent makes everyone that much closer. In my experience, having a single parent was like having one leg: you got used to it, but you always sensed that phantom limb.

"No! I understand everything!"

"Great! I'm glad that's clear!"

I now regret not seeing his generosity for what it was and rebuffing his efforts to open a new door. We've persisted in our mutual games of evasion, but now that I recognize what we're doing, now that I see what we could have been doing instead, I find myself loving him all the more.

The question of why he was leaving had been yanked out of my mind by all that had almost been revealed before I saved us with my cowardice. I remembered only the next day when he said, "See you Sunday" as he dropped me off at the bus stop. At the lot, I read one sentence after another in various textbooks and novels until Ayale visited me in my nest.

"How are you?"

"My father's going away."

"Why?"

Ayale's surprise mirrored my own, for which I was grateful.

"He's visiting people."

"Real people?"

"Exactly."

"Is this the first time he's left you alone?"

"Yup."

"What did you say?"

"Yes."

"Better. Are you going to be all right? You have enough money? You won't get scared?"

"I'll be fine—I'm not five, you know."

"Only the young announce their age at every given opportunity."

Two boys in aviator sunglasses arrived, twins who were starting their own Palestine Liberation Front and wanted Ayale to get involved. We didn't speak again until I said good-bye, while he was giving some last-minute advice to Darius, the younger by three minutes. He offered me a ride, but I declined. I wanted to walk a bit and then sit on a train and then sit on our couch, with no demands to listen and speak. Halfway to the Green Line, I wished I had accepted, and by the time I got home, I felt lonely—surprising since I had been living with someone who sometimes lost his voice from using it so little. I didn't sleep well that night; I had dreams about going to dinner and never coming back out.

The next day, I was drowsing at a nearby café when I started—I thought I'd seen Ayale. I was clearly losing it, gaping at mirages in the middle of Coolidge Corner. I closed my eyes, opened them again, and there he remained, grinning so hard that my face hurt in sympathy.

"What are you doing here?"

"Did you think I lived at the lot, surviving on coffee and newsprint until someone came to relieve me with kind words and stale pastries?"

"No, of course not. But this is nowhere near the lot."

"Did you forget that I still own a car? The kind that can go from one location to another, even when the locations aren't next to each other? I'd even argue that it does better when the locations *aren't* next to each other."

"All right, all right, don't choke on your own cleverness."

Ayale scooped up my mostly intact sandwich and calmly stuck half of it in his mouth. As he chewed, he looked around.

"This is a new place, right?"

"Not at all. Do you like bagels?"

"Not particularly."

"Why are you at a restaurant that only serves bagels?"

"Which is nowhere near the lot that I'm doomed to haunt for the rest of my life."

"Jesus, leave it alone! I'm sorry, okay? You're a vibrant, interested, and interesting person with freedom of movement, freedom of choice, freedom of speech—are you happy now?"

"Why are you getting so irritated?"

"Sorry."

"Do you miss your father?"

"No and no."

"Do you not like being in the house by yourself?"

"It's fine."

"What are you going to do now?"

"Eat lunch."

"You just did."

"*You* just did."

"Right. After your second lunch?"

"Don't know. Movies. Bookstore. I need new sneakers, actually."

"Let's do that last one."

We made our way over to the shoe store I'd been in love with since last year. My father flatly refused to purchase anything from it, stating that it was too expensive and the shoes looked like they would blow apart if one trod too heavily in them.

"They just *look* fragile! They're British!"

"The British should know better. They used to own the world."

In order to enter, one had to pass through the front of a convenience store, where cans of food lined the walls. Bored fashionistas stared at the incoming traffic and sometimes deigned to point people in the direction of the elevator, which led into a magical kingdom of colorful accessories and footwear, although the sneakers were the main attraction.

Ayale looked around with his habitual air of amusement. I showed him two pairs that I had finally decided were my favorites, after a thorough tour of the establishment. Without a word, he took both to the cash register, paid, and gave me the shoeboxes as we exited.

I had become wary of Ayale's munificence. On top of my delivery fees and tips, he continued to gift me with varying amounts of cash, with no warning or reason given. If I tried to refuse, he'd insist, joking that he knew how easily money disappeared when one was young and reckless, apparently not understanding that only one of those adjectives applied to me. My father had already lost his mind when two fifties fell out of my pocket, and I wondered what he'd do when he learned about my delivery gig. He believed these offerings to be near-pathological ways in which Ayale bound people to him, trapping them in a web of debt from which they could never escape. This, according to him, was Ayale's version of creating love. He forbade me from ever accepting anything from Ayale, an empty display of power, which didn't detract from the fact that he was correct. My distrust was born from the fear that Ayale thought he had to keep giving me money to make me stay. I wanted him to understand that I wasn't going anywhere, that I loved him, but since I couldn't get up the courage to say so, the desire felt misbegotten from the start.

I'd like to tell you that I tried to stop Ayale from spending unnecessary money, but let's be honest: I wanted to believe that him buying those shoes proved that he cared. Giving money is impersonal, but a present shows that you know someone. No matter that I'd chosen the shoes. I'd decided this was significant, and I wasn't letting go of that. I thanked him profusely.

"All right, all right. I get nervous when people thank or apologize too much."

"Sorry. No, wait, not sorry. Forget I said that."

We spent the rest of the day in a wandering mode. We stopped when we saw something pretty, something to eat, something to buy, or when we ran out of cigarettes. We talked about my future, as well as *the* future. He explained why silk ties were the only acceptable neckwear, I why *Of Mice and Men* was boring. In this way, it got to a late hour and Ayale drove me back to my apartment. When we arrived, we immediately found an empty parking space; usually my father and I had to circle around the neighborhood for at least fifteen minutes until we could steal into a just-vacated spot, the honking and fuck-yous of other thwarted seekers music to our ears. He kept the engine going as I climbed out and was so neatly ensconced that when I asked him in, there was no extra maneuvering necessary.

He had never before seen the inside of our apartment. He noted that it didn't feel like a basement, and I thanked him as if I had built it myself. I played my father's old records, mostly Ella Fitzgerald. It was almost midnight when he cleared his throat, and I knew that this was the moment we'd been anticipating for most of the day. He wasn't stupid, but neither was I. The sneakers may have been a tactical move on both of our parts.

"I don't know if you remember our little chat. About how a good rule to follow, for the both of us, would be to tell everything there is to tell, whatever that might mean. Do you remember that?"

"Of course I do. It was because of me that we even came up with the rule."

"Let's not forget that it was more that *I* thought of the rule and *you* went along with it—"

"I *agreed* to it; going along with something makes me sound more passive than I'd like."

"I wasn't completely honest with you before."

"Your trust means a lot to me too, thanks."

"I didn't know if I could tell you."

His tone was making me feel panicked; I strove for levity.

"I wonder what else you aren't saying. What about those deliveries? Probably bombs or something like that, huh?"

One look at his face showed me that I'd gone too far. Unbidden, the thought came that if I tried to scream, no one would hear. My father had always viewed the thickness of the walls as a good thing.

"Is that what you really think?"

"No, no, I'm—I'm so—"

"That I'd harm another human being? Any human being?"

"Absolutely not! It was a joke!"

"It's not hard, what you're doing—you know that, right?"

"I didn't mean anything by it! I was messing around, you know me—"

"I thought I did."

He looked like he was trying to locate me in the cosmos of what he knew and cared about.

"I think this is just a misunderstanding."

"I've had about enough of what you think."

We sat in silence, as I sweated and he looked more poised than ever. I cast around in my mind for something that would mend what I'd cracked. My distress must have moved him, or perhaps he'd only been pretending, so that saying what he'd set out to say would have the veneer of forgiveness. Look back on the past, given what you know in the present, and you'll realize that all along, you've been inventing stories and labeling them "history."

"It's about the parking lot."

I almost jumped into his lap, I was so grateful.

"Yes?"

"And I might need your help."

"You'd better start from the beginning."

So he did. And so will I.

It was Ayale who first discovered how to make real money as an attendant. He calculated by how many cars he could surpass the legal limit before actual damage occurred. He discovered that the regulation forty could be stretched to sixty-four or even up to eighty when the weekday security guard for the adjacent office complex was off-duty, since he'd threatened to

report Ayale if he continued to sneak cars over to his section of
the sidewalk. With perfection of the system came increased profits, so that Ayale and his team were usually flying high by Sunday, with Thomas looking the other way as long as he got
4 percent (5 percent with the birth of his second child).

All profits were counted, then divided at the end of the
week, with adjustments made for sick family members, mort-
gage payments, Christmas. The weekly sum had dwindled due
to the rising number of people who had to be given a cut: first
Thomas, then Lentil, then the policeman who did his rounds
in the area, then Elsie ("But that's different," Ayale said, and I
was too scared to ask how), then the two university security
guards who palled around with Ayale when they weren't making greater demands. Luckily, increased sponsorship (as he put
it) had also given them extra parking spaces, their jurisdiction
now covering most of the surrounding streets, even those that
trailed into quiet cul-de-sacs where the wealthy could meet the
same people with the same level of prosperity, over and over
again, until they died in bed.

I didn't know what to say. I didn't grasp how this would
affect me.

"Wow."

"I think that's pretty much all of it."

I would come to regret letting him into our home; it never
felt the same after.

"This is definitely illegal, right?"

"You understand why I have to be careful about who
knows and who doesn't."

"Who else does?"

"Me, the other attendants, their families—most of our
people are aware of it on some level."

"My father?"

"I assume so, yes."

I opened my mouth to see what would come out.

"What is it with you people? You think not getting caught in a lie is the same thing as telling the truth?"

He gave me a look.

"Sorry."

"At least you chose a good movie this time."

"So what happens now?"

Ayale blew out some smoke.

"I don't see myself as someone who will have children. I think you have to be a kind of person that I'm not. I'm glad that you happened onto the lot, I'm glad that you've stayed, and I have no one else of my own to tell. I guess you could say I'm bequeathing this to you; it's my only fortune."

I could have run a marathon: I was absolved.

"Should I be doing something? Is everything going to change?"

He laughed.

"You're safe. But I need you to promise that you won't tell anyone."

"Of course not."

"This isn't a joke. What might seem to you like one car more, one car less, who cares, is more than that to Lentil, to the people who manage Lentil, and to the people who manage the city. I could lose everything I have. And so could everyone else."

"I promise I won't tell anyone."

"This is more than just a promise. This is a covenant. You can't ever break covenants."

"Not like treaties."

"That's why I specifically didn't say 'treaty.' Do you swear to keep this covenant?"

"I solemnly swear."

He looked into me for several seconds before breaking away.

"Good. And now, I'm going home."

"You didn't take a nap today. You must be exhausted."

As he put on his jackets and boots, I struggled for words adequate to all that I felt. He looked back from the doorway.

"Yes?"

I smiled, shook my head, and closed the door.

On the Subject of Distractions

There was no proof that Ayale ever slept with Elsie. True, he had yet to exhibit any qualms whatsoever about sleeping with any woman, single or not, and *true*, such beauty within such easy reach was tempting, especially for the (admittedly) easily waylaid Ayale. No matter. I chose to believe that he remained steadfast, even when confronted with the infamous rose dress, which (admittedly) Elsie did begin to wear almost exclusively on her now daily visits to the lot, to monitor Fiker's recovery she said (never to me), although from what was never explained.

It was Elsie who put her full red lips flush against Fiker's misshapen ear—which no one ever acknowledged—and whispered that Ayale had bigger plans. "Why does he work so hard to get you all that extra money?" "To help us," he replied uncertainly. "Why didn't he help you before? Do you remember how I found you?" He raised a hand to slap her, but she pushed him onto the bed that exacerbated Ayale's back problems, straddling his lumps with her lithe form. "If I were you, I'd stop playing with me and I'd go get what's mine." Fiker still smacked her, to make a point, before struggling into his clothes. It was only a matter of time before envelopes were delivered into her hands, before Ayale was nowhere to be found post-five, pre-seven, before we all started to wonder, then stopped ourselves lest anyone be listening in.

Fiker's presence became an assault; his every move felt like vengeance. He and Ayale laughed louder and louder at each other's jokes, the growing tension causing nosebleeds and head-aches among the attendants. Elsie still visited, but when she did, Ayale stayed in the booth and Fiker spoke to her on the sidewalk, never allowing her onto the lot. There were rumors that one of us had turned informant, sharing secrets with her that were otherwise kept to dead ends and the Greek coffee shop whose grease floated viscously atop all beverages.

I was one of the last to see Elsie before she vanished from the lot—to Montana, said the hopeful; to Eritrea, said the petty. Her magnificent curls were contained in an intricately wrapped scarf. Fiker wasn't there, so Ayale stayed outside, reading the government-sponsored and independent newspapers he received weeks after their publication from Ethiopia, highlighting the portions he felt crucial for my improvement. I hated reading Amharic—it took too long to wrench any sense out of the pro-lix passages of muddy type—but I remained touched by his efforts, proof that I was a worthy person, that my presence in the world mattered.

"Any plans for tonight?" she asked.

"Sleeping."

"Alone?"

She smiled. He didn't.

"Your husband will be back soon."

She waited, arms crossed, and when nothing else came, she shook her head.

"I wouldn't do this if I were you."

He turned a page.

"But you're not."

"If I was, I would have done it better."

He looked at her for a second before throwing his head back for a belly laugh. She turned to leave.

"Tell him I love him."

Ayale shook his head.

"You know how I hate to lie."

This time it was her howls that rang out, long after I'd lost sight of her.

On the Subject of
the Vicissitudes of Telephonic
Communication (II)

After the first couple of weekends my father went away, I became used to his absences. I still felt a hole in the apartment, but this soon gave way to exhilaration each time I walked in and knew that no one else would be entering and then relief when he returned, as if I'd been holding my breath until he came through the door. It was nice to hear his laconic replies and see his mild shock at my enthusiasm as he drifted toward the bookshelf and confirmed that his books were still organized by first name of author, his mind-fuck favorite.

I don't remember when I first noticed his rejuvenation after these weekends. The bloom would fade by the end of the week, when he would sink into colorlessness, indications of life drained away by an insistently wielded syringe. He would pace all night when I told him stories about the lot and so I stopped speaking, because I didn't have anything else. I wasn't angry, and neither was he; we were awash in quiet. We swam easily through our uncommunicativeness and met on the other side with closed-mouth smiles and dry kisses goodnight.

I considered asking him where he went, but in the end I didn't force it. I thought about welcoming him further into my life but forgot to do so when distracted by brighter lights and shinier objects. I regret this now.

There were hints, here and there. He wouldn't yawn as much on Sunday nights, he wouldn't have to slink to bed at an abominably early hour only to wake up still fatigued, dark circles under his eyes, unable to move until I came in with a cup of coffee. He didn't so much gain weight on these weekends as seem more plentiful unto himself, his usual skin-and-bone state alleviated by an inner glow that bestowed upon him the illusion of full-bodied health. He had more opinions on a greater variety of subjects. He knew more questions on *Jeopardy!* when we watched it on Thursday nights, not because it didn't play on other nights, but because that was how he had chosen to do things.

I told Ayale about how my father seemed happy, how maybe all he'd needed was time alone.

"I thought your life with him was constantly contending with his alone time."

"But it's always different when there's someone else there. Even if you're not talking to them, there's a responsibility to act a certain way."

"How do you mean?"

"You won't get naked, you won't speak above a certain volume, you won't open windows or turn on the television without asking, that kind of thing."

"The idea of your father submitting to spontaneous nudity is too much for me."

There was something wrong with the way he said those words. They sounded bitten off, like my fingernails. I chalked it up to his post-Elsie brooding.

My father brought me a shirt from one of his weekends away. It was a surprise, as well as the first actual present I'd received from him since the T pass. (Christmas and birthdays were blank checks, with the understanding that a number above fifty was unacceptable.) The second surprise after the box that was awkwardly pushed toward me was that it contained an aesthetically pleasing item of clothing. We were both embarrassed.

My father became obsessed with his failings as my father. He began to watch me more closely. He asked questions which required long explanations, he asked questions to which he should have already known the responses, he asked questions which revealed more about him than about me, he asked questions that I didn't want to answer.

"What's your favorite color?"

"Do you like school?"

"How many languages do you speak?"

"What *is* the difference between violets and hyacinths?"

"Do you get enough sunshine, on a regular basis?"

"Do you shave your legs yet?"

"What's the capital of Madagascar?"

"Do you like me?"

"Do you love me?"

"You don't have to answer if you don't want to."

"Do you love Ayale?"

"Please answer me."

He suddenly couldn't hear enough about Ayale. He sought out information about the lot, laughed at my retellings of Ayale's jokes, even promised to visit him. I was skeptical of and pleased by his interest, never mind that it sometimes felt like I had to channel someone else in order to be of note to my own father.

Appropriately enough, Ayale began to disappear around this time. He barely gave me the courtesy of listening noises when I conscientiously provided him with pauses in the stream of chatter that had become my trademark, nudges to push him out of the secret place to which he was withdrawing and from which I felt barred. It's painful to be aware of how unwelcome your presence is to someone you love and to nevertheless be incapable of the dignified act of removing yourself. It's even worse when Fiker is smirking at you from behind your loved one's shoulder, when your loved one is so preoccupied that it's Fiker who gives you the boxes to be delivered, Fiker who pays you, his bills somehow always dirtier than Ayale's.

"You have a lot to say lately?"

He grinned, taking a few seconds too long to release the money into my hands.

"Why do you dislike me so much?"

His eyes widened. Elsie had been gone for weeks, and his appearance had deteriorated accordingly.

"I think you're wonderful."

"Then why is everything changing?" I was dangerously close to wailing.

"This is what you're having trouble with? This part? This is nothing. I *live* in this part."

I wouldn't have wished any of it upon my worst enemy. In elementary school, the girls knew that you truly hated something when you swore to God that you wouldn't wish it upon someone they knew to be your mortal foe. It was a Catholic school, so we had limited resources.

We started to receive phone calls. The phone had become a

forgotten artifact in our apartment; Ayale had long ago stopped calling, and we didn't have other friends. Suddenly, however, it wouldn't stop ringing. It would shock me awake, cause me to fall in the shower as I ran to catch it, make me late as I flew back inside after I'd already locked the door. I was so accustomed to the phone being the harbinger of emergency or Ayale that I would kill myself to get to it before it was silenced by the unknown at the other end.

The other person never spoke or hung up. I eventually stopped saying hello and just listened to the breathing. It was a friendly moment. I felt this person meant no harm. Nevertheless, each time I walked into the apartment and saw my father opening windows, lighting cigarettes, shaking macaroni boxes, not once near the phone, I wondered who the person was in pursuit of.

I finally began to speak, mentioning specific people as if the other person knew them, and slowly, it began to feel as if he or she did. Good listeners are hard to find.

"I tried to get into an advanced art class today, but they told me I had no skill. I guess that makes sense, because I've never taken a beginning art class. But in French I made up a character named Monsieur Fromage whose head is a spiral. *Fromage* means cheese."

"Sorry I didn't answer your first call—I was trying to rub feeling back into my hands."

"I auditioned for the play, but goddamn Liz was there and she wears all black and has spiky hair, so she'll probably get the part. They'll probably change the whole thing into a one-woman show about how spiky her hair is."

"I don't like tank tops."

"I don't like the third floor."

"The Ethiopian cell-phone guy at Prudential is gone. They took away his kiosk and everything."

"I think I'm going to write a story about my mother and call it 'Adoption.'"

"What do *you* think of my father?"

"I have a crush on Ben. He says ridiculous things in English class."

"I have a crush on Bryan. He says ridiculous things in biology class."

I brought up the litany of silent calls to my father, and he stayed quiet as I laughingly speculated on the caller's motives.

"It's probably the FBI, tapping our phone lines."

I waited for him to continue the game and, when he didn't, prodded him along.

"I bet it's a runaway, hungering for human affection. Or maybe we're victims of a hate crime. Or we're at the mercy of a serial killer. Oh my God. This is that movie with Rain Phoenix combined with the one where Mel Gibson is a kidnapper."

"It's Michael Douglas, and he doesn't kidnap anyone. No on the other counts, too."

He clearly didn't understand the rules of my game, so I tried playing his significantly less fun one.

"How do you know?"

"Do you talk to her when she's on the phone with you?"

"Not a lot. Do you ... um ... talk to her?"

"I've never answered the phone."

"I'm not making it up, you know."

"I know."

"Why do you know?"

"I just do."

"Should I stop answering the phone?"

"Of course not. That's what you're supposed to do when the phone rings: you answer it."

"Right, but . . . do we know this person? Should I be delivering a message?"

"I don't think so."

I wasn't sure if this was an answer to one or both of the questions.

"So why does she keep calling? If it's a she, I mean."

"I don't know."

He didn't appear to be lying, but I still didn't believe him.

When I told Ayale about the phantom calls, he shrugged, an action he usually decried. With so many mysteries crowding my life, I decided to solve this one right here, right now. The man wasn't going to shrug at me and get away with it, heartbreak be damned.

"Is something wrong?" I asked.

"I don't understand; weren't you just telling me that something was wrong?"

"So you *were* listening? That's good to know, because I honestly couldn't tell."

"So there *is* something wrong."

"Are you . . . angry at me?"

Ayale crossed his arms and looked past me, somewhere far above my head, before abruptly crouching to speak to me, eye to eye.

"Your delightful, lit-up-from-within father has come on three separate occasions, just in the past week. Did you know that?"

I was having trouble maintaining eye contact but was determined not to break it, not to lose him again.

"No."

"He came to have a chat with me. The first time, I was more

than happy to see him; families of friends are friends of mine. I got him some coffee. I gave him the chair in the booth. I asked if he'd eaten. He was my guest."

"What happened?"

I felt dizzy, and when the words came out of my mouth, they sounded different than usual.

"He asks me if I'm not ashamed of myself. For what, I ask. For leading on an impressionable young girl. I should know better, there can be nothing healthy in such a close relationship between a man and a young girl—he's fond of that phrase, your father, 'young girl'—and the more he observes your behavior at home, the more sure of this he is. I ask him what about your behavior he's noticed. He says you've changed, completely, that nine out of ten sentences are about me. I say I'm flattered but I don't see the harm. Wouldn't it have been the same if you'd become besotted with a movie star? Wouldn't he rather you choose someone who can improve you? He replies that the movie star would be quickly forgotten. I'm actually here, I can't be erased that quickly. I ask him if that's what he wants to do, erase me. He says he wouldn't mind. I ask him why, and he says he's never liked me. He says that if everyone was being honest, they'd remember that love and fascination are two different emotions. Then he leaves. Our conversations on the next two occasions are shorter and end with another phrase your father adores: 'stay away from my daughter.'"

I was shaking and sat on the ground, humiliated. My father had actually told Ayale, in so many words, that I was obsessed with him, and Ayale seemed not only to believe this but to have taken it for granted. I was not obsessed. What I felt was so much more. He was making it seem like spending time with me was a favor, a way for me to accrue knowledge, but the joke was on him: I didn't remember where the Mediterranean was or if Russia was in Europe or Asia. I hated my father for butting in, for taking over my life like I was something small enough to step over. I hated Ayale for pointing out his merits as a role model without mentioning that maybe he would miss me. I didn't want either of them. *They* were the children, cock fighting in the afternoon.

Ayale stood up.

"Maybe we should suspend our little package system. Give you some time to recover."

I propelled myself into a standing position and hauled ass to Government Center, almost breaking my nose when I tripped over my own feet and smashed my face into the ground. There was nothing left. I had prepared myself for my father leaving, but never Ayale. I'd thought you could lose only two parents. Soon I'd have just Fiker, which was tantamount to having no one.

I didn't speak to my father after that. I would stare him down as he attempted to initiate communication, until he withdrew into his room. He began leaving plates of food on the table and going to bed as soon as he came home from work. I still went to the lot but left earlier and earlier, hoping that Ayale would ask where I was going, miserable each time he didn't. He might or might not have called during this period, but since I'd stopped answering the phone, I wouldn't know. My body always hurt. Classes were extended sessions of physical torture; I emerged drenched in sweat, hoping no one could smell or see me.

I bought headphones, but even music was distressing. Instead, I would listen to the phone ring and ring and ring. It took a while, but finally, whoever it was stopped calling.

ON THE SUBJECT OF HOW WE GOT INVOLVED

Sisay and Nathan were dumped in front of the Dunkin' Donuts on Boylston Street. The first had stab wounds in his chest and stomach; the second nothing but a stunned expression and an empty wallet. The brothers had been working at a small Alewife lot for nearly five years. Sisay had recently gotten married with a lot of fanfare, while Nathan had to be dragged out of bars to make his morning shifts. They had been spotted loudly fighting right before their corpses were discovered. Their mother was convinced that the source of the evil was the washing machine they had forced upon her.

When three taxi drivers were found dead a month later, we started to connect the dots. According to Ayale, the deaths had been happening for years. Kassahun was the first I'd heard of, but there'd been others before him, spread out over months. The recent murders that had blended into the background of my life were part of a greater, more sinister design. The latest three had been baptized by the same priest in a forgotten corner of Jima, all young, all pooling their money to invest in a building venture on the outskirts of Addis Ababa, which was now running their obituaries in its official newsletter, free of charge.

Once Ayale had revealed the existence of a pattern, we had him review the chronology again and again, to make sure we understood. He was patient and even offered to write it all down, but that seemed a step too far. It was clear that he was the only one who could help us, not least because of all the information he scrounged up, details whose provenance we didn't question, so relieved were we to have them. The usual number of people clustered around his booth quadrupled. Initially, they tried for discretion, but the need to know became too great and everyone crowded around, silent, immobile. Ayale handled the growing throngs and the parked cars with an ease that bordered on joy. Chaos brought out the best in him. He thrived on the fear of others. He had never been so attentive. I felt guilty about my gratitude to the deceased for returning him to me, disgusted at myself for releasing my anger so easily, and certain that all too soon, I'd lose him again.

We thought that Ayale would be the one to crack the case. According to him, the police were at a loss as to who the murderer was, what his motives might be, how he was even getting at the men, since autopsies put their times of death early enough that the streets wouldn't yet be empty. Many of them had been with others up until these projected times, and yet their friends had noticed nothing amiss. According to Ayale, the police hadn't even linked these recent deaths with the previous ones until he came on the scene. It hadn't escaped them that all of the victims were Ethiopian men under the age of thirty-five; Ayale made sure of that. When asked if he was in contact with the specific detectives on the case, he pursed his lips enigmatically, as if his role was too vast to be explained. We respected his reserve so deeply that we questioned him all the more. His cloak-and-dagger responses didn't deter us; his mere presence made us feel safe. I began to call him before I went to bed, and I could tell that this pleased him.

With the exception of the brothers, none of the men were overtly connected. None were extraordinary, either in our community or the American one which made ours possible. None of them had children, not even illegitimate ones back home. Taxi drivers and parking lot attendants began to band together at night, refusing to leave well-lit and well-populated areas. Ethiopians started seeking out Americans, since none of the victims had been accompanied by non-Ethiopians. Bostonians became good-luck charms. Ayale told me to bring people to the lot, just in case, but I didn't want to introduce anyone new; I was afraid that they would love him not enough or too much. I scoffed that the murderer clearly had no interest in women. The minute I said "murderer," I felt I had thrown a grenade into the world that I could never call back.

I was curious as to how Ayale knew all that he did about the crimes. I finally asked when we were able to escape the gaggle of people around his booth. The groups had begun to thin out during the long period of clenched quiet directly preceding the fifth taxi driver's demise. They had become resigned and, what's more, had begun to suspect. Not Ayale necessarily, but something which made it seem wiser to pull back. I didn't tell him.

"I listen. You'd be surprised at how much information is dropped here and there."

"At police headquarters, sure."

"You just have to be in the right places at the right times."

"Not like Kassahun, huh? Wrong place, wrong time. Remember?"

The streets surrounding us were deserted. Everyone was at work or getting killed. He put his hand on my shoulder.

"It's going to be okay, you'll see. Come on, you're a city girl—this stuff is nothing."

"Why won't you tell me how you know?"

Ayale's grip tightened.

"Why should I?"

"Because."

"Because what?"

"All of us just want to know, that makes sense."

"But why are *you* specifically asking *me*, right now?"

"Let go, that hurts!"

"Answer me!"

"Because I'm afraid!"

"Of what?"

"Of you!"

He gripped me a second longer. When I looked into his eyes, I saw that he could never understand why one might feel fear in the face of the unknown, in the face of death, in the face of seeing only death and the unknown in the eyes of someone you love.

"One of the usual police officers couldn't come to the lot for his payment, so I went by the station. That was right after Kassahun. I saw how useful this could be and offered to keep coming back with the money so that he wouldn't have to tire himself out, and he was almost on his knees, that's how grateful he was. It was pathetic."

I couldn't respond; my mouth was devoid of language. Ayale walked into the booth and shut the door. I sat on the ground and placed my head on my knees, to the concern of all who hovered or worked. Someone put his hands on my head, a woman's voice asked if I wanted some tea, and I felt buoyed up by them, as if my loss paralleled theirs and so we grieved on the same plane, within the same dimensions.

Ayale woke me when his ride arrived. My ass hurt from sitting on the ground. When I tried to get into the car, he pushed me back.

"Have a good night."

"But—"

"It's probably better if you go on your own, without me. Just in case."

"I don't know what came over me, I was just so scared—"

"I don't have time for this."

"Don't you ever lose perspective and say something you don't really mean? Has that never happened to you?"

"No."

"No?"

"No."

"You're lucky. You would never have been as stupid as I was."

"Let's not make a scene here."

The driver was staring straight ahead, but I knew this didn't mean he wasn't also intently listening, eager to deliver the gossip as soon as he could get away.

I tried not to cry as Ayale stepped into the car, as he shut the door, as they drove away. At home, I looked at my father's door, wishing I could talk to him, but knew that I had nothing to say, not yet.

ON THE SUBJECT OF LOOKING AROUND CORNERS

I waited a week so that Ayale would know how definitively furious I was; to let the fact that I wasn't a permanent fixture in his life sink in; to show him that not only could I leave but I might very well prefer it; to demonstrate that I, a person with a mind full to bursting with non-Ayale-related matters, when insulted, belittled, or threatened had a sense of self that was so healthy that I would, without question, abandon any who dared carry out psychological violence unto me. It would be stating the obvious to say that I wasn't a doormat because I lived my saturated-with-prospects existence in a way that was defiantly un-doormat-like: let those with eyes see.

The week was supposed to accomplish all this and more, except that I couldn't stop watching *The Way We Were*, weeping each time Hubbell and Katie laid eyes on each other at the hotel, exasperated with myself at each viewing. The years immediately preceding exile found me extremely concerned about wasting time, despite quickly learning that I didn't do much. This became painfully evident during my parking lot abstinence. I went to school every day but, inexplicably, classes were getting easier, so despite my prolific note-taking and diligent homework-doing, all my educational obligations were complete by early after-noon. I had already phased out extracurriculars because they would have cut into my lot time, and it was too late in the year to join anything except Latin Club, whose two members never showed up at the reserved classroom. Time seemed like a gift from someone who kept asking if I liked it, propelling me into greater depths of guilt as I saw it gather dust in a drawer.

By Monday of the next week, I had planned everything: the precise time of my arrival and departure, what I would say, how I would act. It was crucial not to linger; I didn't need him or anyone else to think that I'd missed him. I would be polite but reserved. I'd bring some of my new books, mostly tomes on African political policy, all of which bored me but which I felt displayed to those who cared—it was undeniable that he cared—that I was more than capable of keeping up with mod-ern intellectual thought (I needed it to be undeniable, and thus I equated "need" with "fact") and certainly didn't require spoon-fed instruction. I dawdled after school. I went to the bathroom. I checked in on Latin Club. I bought chips. I went to the bathroom again.

There were the usual bevies of people in every corner of the lot. No one looked at me, and it was the screaming from behind the closed booth door that made me draw closer.

"You're going about this all wrong," Fiker's voice announced.

"Have you seen yourself? Have you seen your life?"

Fury seemed to be making it difficult for Ayale to get the words out.

"I just want to help!"

"What help could you *possibly* give?"

Ayale sounded genuinely curious.

"You need an extra person! You think that priest is going to stick around forever? And if you tell me what's going on, I can—"

"You can *what*? What can you contribute? You needed Elsie just to know this much!"

"You shut your mouth about Elsie."

Fiker's rage made my heart beat faster and faster, as if it were aimed at me.

"You're worse now than when you first came," Ayale said, more quietly.

"You can't do it by yourself."

"I've *always* done it by myself. You're the one who always needs people. Ever since we were kids, you've *needed* so much."

"I wonder what your mother would think of that statement."

"Watch it."

"She didn't know what you'd done. If it weren't for you, she'd still—"

"Wait."

Footsteps before the door banged open on an Ayale who looked ready to kill.

"Can I help you?"

I waited for more and, when it wasn't forthcoming, wriggled my way past him into the booth. He followed my progress as Fiker leaned against the back wall with an attitude just missing casual.

"How long were you standing there?"

"I just got here," I lied.

Ayale didn't seem convinced. We stood in silence, seemingly waiting for something, although what that something was or if it was the same for all of us was anyone's guess. I finally pulled a cigarette from my jacket pocket, installed it in the corner of my mouth, and gazed back and forth before directing my request to a point in the middle.

"Could I borrow a lighter?"

No response. Ayale sat in his usual chair and plucked a magazine from the floor. Fiker looked too weak to stand upright without the support of the booth. I took a breath before launching into my prepared speech.

"I'd like to apologize for disappearing. I imagine that you'd also like to apologize, so why don't we just—"

"If I give you a lighter, will you go?" Ayale's voice was muffled by the hand he was now leaning on. He had yet to turn a page.

Worry was entrenching itself in my gut, turning into the kind of panic that I felt on Sundays when my father arrived later than usual. I swiftly took measures to cut it off before it colonized my insides, choking any ability to think clearly, make smart decisions, not lose him.

"No, I will not leave if you give me the lighter."

I smiled but stopped when I found that I was the only one.

"What will you do?" he wondered aloud.

"We will talk and make things right."

"Nothing is wrong, so there's no need for that. You can go."

It was his turn to smile alone.

"I'm truly sorry," I whispered. "I said things I didn't mean. Maybe you did, too."

"I never say what I don't mean."

"Debatable," murmured Fiker, eyes shut.

Ayale glared in his direction.

"Please forgive me. Please. I'm sorry."

"No need to be sorry, nothing to forgive. I've told you before that I don't like excessive thanks and apologies."

"Also debatable."

Both of us glared at Fiker.

"Can I help you?" I snapped.

Fiker opened his eyes and looked at me, a closed-mouthed sneer peeking out.

"You have no quarrel with me."

"I have no quarrel with anyone!"

Ayale jumped in.

"Which means you can light your cigarette and be on your way!"

"If you're not angry, why are you kicking me out?"

He tore his eyes away from the magazine.

"Why would you stay? You don't work here."

"What about *him*?" I asked, jabbing a finger in Fiker's direction. "What's his official position, Ayale? What purpose does *he* serve?" I jerked my hand toward the others, whose eyes were occupied beholding matters and objects that were nowhere near our vicinity. "What about *them*? I see"—I did a swift count—"two attendants. The rest are just *here*. Shall I inform them that they're no longer wanted?"

He hurled the magazine onto the floor but kept his voice level.

"I think it would be easier if you just told me what you want."

"I only—"

"Keep your voice down."

The end of my cigarette was damp and disgusting; I pulled it out, trying not to cry.

"I'd like for things to go back to the way they were."

"And how were they before? In your opinion?"

"We were friends."

He nodded very seriously.

"I see. What made you think we were friends?"

"We spent time together, I helped you with things, you helped me, too."

He nodded again.

"Come here."

I knew I shouldn't hope, but I did. I looked down at his face, his increasingly veiny eyes, the mole on his cheek. He took my hand, indicating with his other the walls of the booth.

"How could we be friends? I'm a parking lot attendant. You're a child."

"You're more than an attendant."

"Am I?" He turned my hand over and stared at the palm. "America gave me a job, which means it gave me a name—the attendant—and an identity—the man who parks cars—and a purpose—to park as many cars as possible. That's all. Everything else, you need to forget. And before that, you need to leave."

To say that I spent the next few days in a haze would imply that I had a self which could experience things like alertness and stupor. I must have displaced my body from one location to another because my journal entries, faithfully kept, detail class incidents, quotes, successfully completed assignments, confirmations of my father's presence. I am only eyes in these entries, reporting on people and places, providing not a clue as to how they affected me. There was no "me" to affect. I only needed to breathe enough air so that I could keep records on those still capable of living.

It was while walking from the bus to my apartment during

this stretch of nothing that I felt someone behind me. When I turned, no one was there. At one time, I might have found this alarming, but now I was concerned only with getting inside as quickly as possible and hastening the hours until sleep. I hadn't gone far when I espied someone checking a parking meter on the opposite sidewalk; I was sure that he'd been staring at me a second earlier. I watched more closely, and to his credit, he feigned absorption for a little longer before briskly walking toward the corner gas station. Someone coughed. I looked over only to be confronted with a neighbor whose name I forgot but who always said hi because we'd bought appliances from one of her stoop sales.

"How you doin', honey?"

"Fine, thanks, yourself?"

"Can't complain, can't complain."

I waited.

"Funniest thing, that man."

"Which one?"

"The one you were lookin' at."

"What about him?"

I didn't mean to sound testy, but it had been a good long while since anyone besides my father had addressed me, and I had lost the little practice I'd gained.

"He's been monkeyin' around with that meter for a minute now."

"How long exactly?"

"Oh, I don't know—I been sittin' here since two and it's four-thirty now and he's been there the whole time *I* been here. But I don't know, maybe he got there sooner—"

"What *exactly* has he been doing? Can you tell me?"

"Sure, honey." She took a sip of something that smelled like ginger. "He plays with the meter, same as you saw, walks away for a bit, gets in his car for a bit, plays with the meter for a bit. Over and over and over until you came, and now he's gone."

Her complacency irritated me, as did the fear that was starting to climb into my throat. Why was I scared? I wasn't special. Never had been.

"You've seen him before?"

She shook her head no. "You'd recognize him if I did, y'all been living here long enough."

I wanted nothing more than to be inside, all doors locked, multiple cigarettes inhaled before my father came home.

"Thank you, ma'am."

"You take care now, baby."

I could see our front door and was just about to turn onto the stairs when someone bumped into me, hard enough that I fell onto my backpack and the two textbooks I'd been holding went flying into the street. The culprit was slight; I was surprised at her strength. She apologized, picked up my books, repeatedly asked if I was all right.

"You're going home?"

I nodded.

"Right here?"

I nodded and instantly knew that I'd made a mistake.

"Well, actually—"

"Sorry again."

She was already approaching the neighbor, who looked at me tranquilly.

"You okay, honey?"

I bolted inside. When I heard my father arrive, I debated with myself for a moment before realizing that if I didn't speak, I wasn't going to make it. I walked to meet him and found that I didn't remember how to start. He cleared his throat.

"Mona's sitting outside pretty late."

"Who's Mona?"

"You know, that neighbor we bought the little fridge from."

"She's still there?" I screeched.

"Oh, she was here when you arrived?"

"Why else would I say *still*?"

All my dread, my hoping that I was crazy, was pummeling him. He looked shocked and then the saddest I'd ever seen him.

"Did I do something wrong," I heard him say, but I was already in my room, under the covers, waiting for sleep or a polite stranger to silence me, whichever came first.

On the Subject of
How the Answer Was Worse

The meter man was on the morning bus, a couple loitered outside my school for the entirety of first-period chemistry, and I could have sworn the woman who pushed me was standing in the usual mob around the wrap truck; by the time I ran over, she was gone.

Two weeks had passed since the originally planned one-week absence when I finally went to see Ayale. The lot looked neither better nor worse. Ayale seemed haggard, and when I asked after his health, he curtly replied that he wasn't the only one not sleeping. I was unsure what this meant, but knew I didn't have much time.

"People are following me and I don't know why."

He didn't hesitate.

"Tell me exactly what happened."

When I'd finished, he poked his head out of the booth. Seconds later, Fiker shut the door behind himself.

"Tell him," Ayale ordered as he motioned for Fiker to sit down, so I did.

Fiker took a toothpick out of his pocket and stuck it in his mouth.

"What do you think?" Ayale asked him.

I absently wondered if arguments like the one I'd heard were common occurrences. This idea pleased me.

"You know what I think."

"I don't," I said loudly. No one told me to keep my voice down.

Ayale gave me a long look.

"Come, stand next to me."

He took my hand the way he had before, except now it felt like homecoming.

"You *do* know." He said this gently. "You know every-thing."

"Tell me anyway."

"Some officers on our payroll have been warning us that their bosses are keeping a closer eye on them. My guess is, while it's harder to trail the others or us, you're an easy target. They're just making sure you're not doing anything illegal, which, of course, you aren't."

"And you never were," Fiker added.

"So . . . they're police officers?"

Both men nodded.

"Most likely."

"Wait, but . . . how long will they follow me?"

Ayale threw up his hands.

"That's not for either of us to say. But it's obvious that our

people have to get involved. I'm not going to let you just walk around by yourself, with I don't know how many cops watching your every move."

"What happened to not being friends?"

He looked blank before allowing a small smile. It took me a few minutes to register what he'd said.

"How will your people get involved?"

"They'll have to follow you, too." He shushed me with a gesture. "It's the only way to guarantee your safety. We need people *we* trust to make sure that *they* don't do anything crazy. Or, at least, nothing crazier than what they've already done."

Nothing about this plan made me feel better. I didn't see how a ragtag team of amateur Ethiopian spies was going to outwit and—if it came down to it—overpower trained police officers. I didn't want more shadow people. And what if my father inquired into the sudden influx of random bystanders on our block?

"It'll mean that you'll have to stop coming here." He noticed my expression. "For a little while. Just long enough to throw them off the scent."

I still didn't say anything, and my silence clearly started to bother Ayale, who looked skittish for the first time since I'd known him.

"It's not perfect, but it's the only way, at least for now. You won't even know they're there."

The rising impatience in his voice gave me pause. I had missed him, there was no denying it, but distance had made me realize, more ferociously than before, that while Ayale was a great many things, a good man was not one of them.

Both of his hands were on my shoulders now, pressing down, allowing no movement.

"There's no other way to protect you. Or your father."

I finally nodded, and only then did he let me go. I made as if to leave.

"Where are you going? Don't you have homework?"

"But I thought you said . . ."

"You're already here, aren't you? You haven't gotten lazy on me, have you?"

What could I do? I treasured being on the same side as him. I laughed when he laughed, and already I felt lighter, less trapped than minutes before.

"Never."

"Then get to it! I have to go make sure total mayhem hasn't taken over."

It was as I scanned the booth for a corner into which I could cram my backpack that I saw the postcard. Someone had drawn a beach on it, with a woman close to the shore. It brought to mind my mother's word "loneless," meaning without a home and alone, and how it was only in middle school that I had learned, to my shame, that it wasn't a real word. It brought to mind something else as well, but before I could pin it down, Fiker had already swung forward, yanked the postcard from where it had been stuck, and stuffed it into one of his pockets.

"Let me see it."

If he was surprised by my tone, he didn't show it.

"It's rude to snoop."

"I wasn't snooping."

"Would you like to discuss it with *him*?"

Fiker laughed when I turned, thinking Ayale was there. I improvised.

"I have the same postcard."

He smirked.

"Oh *really*? So you and Ayale have the same friends? What a coincidence!"

I was reduced to pleading.

"Just let me see it. Please."

I could tell, from the extreme wrinkle of his brow and the absurdly acute tilt of his head that his serious thought was only pretense. He shook his head in defeat.

"I can't find it."

"Fiker! It's in your pocket!"

Ayale appeared in the doorway.

"What's going on?"

Fiker carefully stuck his toothpick behind his ear.

"She had a question, I think. For you."

Ayale looked at me.

"What?"

"Nothing," I whispered.

Fiker yawned.

"I'd better get going." He looked toward me. "Welcome back, by the way."

ON THE SUBJECT OF NEW YEAR PRESENTS

When the phone rang next, it was already September again. My father and I were celebrating the Ethiopian New Year by drinking coffee in separate rooms. It had been so long since I'd last seen our phone act like the instrument it was bought to be that it took four calls for me to finally remember that I had a part to play as well.

"Hello?"

"I need you to come to the lot tomorrow morning at seven."

Per his instructions, I'd barely seen Ayale since the beginning of the summer. Everything had felt charged since the postcard; circumstances had taken on edges that threatened to maim. I still felt his presence, in the men I saw skulking around the neighborhood, studiously avoiding my gaze, my supposed

Secret Service. Hearing his voice made me miss him all over again.

"I have to go to school—"

"Before school."

"My father will ask questions."

"Make something up."

I'd almost forgotten that his requests were our commands. I started to miss him just a little bit less.

"Like—tutoring?"

"For example."

"Okay."

"You will be here?"

"I'll figure something out."

"That doesn't answer my question."

"I'll be there."

He'd already hung up.

Later, while eating pasta with mushroom sauce, I told my father that I had to take an earlier bus to school the next day. Ever since my uneasy reconciliation with Ayale, I'd allowed conversation to flourish in our apartment, although guilt at my father's relief and eagerness to take up where we had left off prevented me from feeling any kind of joy. I think I was glad, though.

"First of all, thank you for setting the table."

Our last year of living in the basement was marked by a distinct increase in courtesy, as if to stave off even the slightest chance of conflict.

"You're welcome."

"Second of all, I could drive you."

"I don't want to make you wake up that early."

"I don't mind."

"That's very nice of you. Thank you."

"You're welcome."

"But, you know, I get sick when I read in cars, and I need to review my notes for the session."

"Who's tutoring you?"

"My teacher."

"That's nice of her."

"She's a nice lady."

"She sounds like it."

"She is."

It was decided, both that I would go by myself and that this teacher was of upstanding moral stock.

I saw him hesitate before he timidly asked, "Is everything all right?"

Since Ayale's call, I kept forgetting to breathe, which meant that every so often, I'd find myself gasping for air. Even if my father wasn't my first choice for advice, he'd have to do.

"In general, do you go with what you feel now or what you've felt before?"

He thought about this.

"Between instinct and history, I guess I'd go with history."

"But is that the right thing to do?"

He smiled.

"I guess that depends."

"On what?"

"On how badly or how well you think I've turned out."

It was my turn to hesitate.

"Well—"

He started clearing the plates.

"I'd rather you didn't say, if you don't mind. Thank you."

When I arrived at the lot the next morning, I had brushed my teeth twice, changed my outfit so many times that I didn't actually remember what I was wearing, and stolen a pack from my father.

"I hope I'm not too late."

Ayale looked at me as if I were a cockroach.

"It's six forty-five."

"Right."

He handed me four gift-wrapped packages, each tied with curly red ribbon and displaying a New Year's card, the same picture of happy children with yellow flowers that has always been used, no matter how many more adorable children and yellow flowers are created.

"You need to take these to the addresses that I've written, here in the corner, and you need to do it by noon."

I nodded vigorously to show him with what energetic zeal I was comprehending, though I recognized none of the streets.

"How's all this going, by the way?"

"How's all *what* going?"

He checked his watch, which I noticed was silver and beautifully filigreed. It was the first time I'd seen him wear anything at the lot that hinted at money.

"The package system for relatives, is it going well?"

His bewilderment confirmed what I'd only guessed.

"I haven't delivered anything for a while, so I thought maybe you didn't have as much coming through anymore."

"Can we talk about this later? You'll be late for school, and some of this is time-sensitive."

He consulted his watch again.

"You told me at the diner."

Understanding dawned on his face.

"Yes. Yes. Of course. I must need a vacation." He shook his head, as if in wonder at his own stupidity. "I wanted you to focus on your college applications, so I just had the others drop them off. They weren't as efficient as you, but they were cheaper!"

I couldn't stop staring at his mobile features, marveling at his effortless cheer, shrinking away from the performance. He tapped me on the cheek.

"What's wrong?"

"You're lying."

He looked surprised, and his accurate aping of the emotion both intrigued and repelled me.

"How am I lying?"

"What you're saying doesn't make any sense; the attendants could have done the deliveries this whole time. Why pay me? And if it was true about the people in Ethiopia, the relatives who send gifts or whatever, how could you have forgotten? And we've never talked about my applications!"

He looked amused.

"It slipped my mind—that happens when you get older. And of course I've been thinking about your college plans. I care about you."

My hands were starting to shake, so I carefully placed the boxes on the pavement.

"What's in them?"

"Presents from relatives," he promptly replied.

"Tell me the truth."

"I am telling you the truth."

"No, you're not."

He sighed.

"If that's what you think, that's what you think. Will you deliver these or not?"

"Tell me what's in them."

"I've already told you."

He began gathering up the boxes. I grabbed one from him and clutched it to my chest.

"Fine, then just tell me this: will I get hurt if I deliver them?"

"Who gets hurt for giving presents to people?"

"Why didn't you ask an attendant? Am I more expendable?"

He whistled. "Fiker told me that you seemed spooked, but I didn't believe him until now."

I persisted. "No one's been killed for a while now."

"Don't tell me that upsets you?"

"Why me? Why now?"

"I'm starting to get angry. We've already gone over this."

"Whose side are you on?"

He looked at me. After weeks of being examined from afar by strangers too discreet to do so beyond predetermined intervals, it felt breathtaking to be truly seen by someone, even if the person in question was too terrifying for me to be able to look back. I aimed my gaze at his right ear.

"I'm leaving soon," he said, as if this explained it all.

"What?"

"I'll be gone in a year. Maybe two."

"Why?"

He thought about this.

"I've been here for over thirty years. Most people I know have become citizens, have kids; they've settled into a routine, decided they're American. I wondered if I should do the same, but then I realized: it's all a game. The first round is making it over here; the second is getting papers, then learning English, then a job, then lasting long enough to save money, then getting credit cards, falling into debt, over and over again. And after all that, what do you get? *Maybe* a passport. You work so hard, you pay taxes, you laugh at their famine jokes, you support their foreign policies, you turn your back on your own people, to be *like them*, and your reward is, you get to pretend that you're *just like them*, even though none of *them* would blink if you were cut down in the street." He indicated the lot with his hands. "Do you realize that I'm supposed to see all of this as a favor? That I'm supposed to be ashamed of the little extra I make on the side, even though without it, none of us would survive?"

"I'm not really sure—"

"Don't get me wrong: I've learned a lot. I've studied their system. And I've realized that by staying here, I'm helping them but not helping *us*. I need to start something of my own and not just join in someone else's dream. Does that make sense?"

"Well . . . yes."

"I'm telling you this because I think it's important for you to get your own dream, too."

"What do you mean?"

"Get out of Boston. Forget about people getting killed, parking lots. Do what you want to do."

"But this *is* what I want to do. More or less."

"Maybe now it's less. And maybe you're right."

We looked at each other.

"You're not expendable. If anyone ever tells you that, you kill them first."

I picked up the boxes before I spoke.

"Can we talk more about all of this? Soon?"

"Of course."

He kissed me on the cheek and waved when I looked back.

I'd like to think that I knew he was lying, but he wasn't wrong: things do slip my mind more and more.

The first address was just off the huge billboard at Blue Hill and Morton, after the onslaught of single-floor churches that trumpeted JESUS SAVES and LORD CHRIST'S SACRED BLOOD from dirt-encrusted neon signs. It was a two-family home, painted two different colors. A woman answered the door after an elaborate symphony of chimes.

"Who are you?"

"I have something for you."

She crossed her arms and looked me up and down.

"I've heard about you."

"I told you, I have to give you something."

"So give it to me."

I handed over her present. She took a look at it, snorted, and then went back to her appraisal of my person. She didn't seem impressed.

"Is there anything else?"

"Have a nice day?"

The door was already shutting in my face.

The next two addresses were near each other on Columbia Road. At both, a man answered, thanked me, and was gone before I could so much as finish a full cycle of respiration. At the fourth apartment, I put my foot in the door as soon as it started to draw back and asked for a glass of water. When I looked up from the package, I saw Fiker. He seemed amused at my shock as he opened the door wider. He waited until I'd finally decided to enter, indicated the plastic-covered couch which ruled the living room, and shuffled into the kitchen. I had drunk two glasses before I thanked him. I wondered, as I often did, how long it had been since he'd last bathed.

"Your eyes look red."

"I didn't sleep much last night."

"Sure you weren't crying?"

"Why would I cry?"

I tried to glare, but in his eyes I saw all of the reasons why I might and looked away. He grinned as I made a big show of putting down the glass, brushing off my lap—from the crumbs in the water, don't you know—and getting up.

"I'd better go."

"No, stay a minute. I'm your last, right?"

"I need to get to school. If I sign in after eleven, they'll mark me absent, not tardy."

"God. Why does this education system choose to dabble in nonsensical bureaucracy?"

"I don't know."

He was the only person who spoke to me in English. He had no accent, but his choice of words marked him as hopelessly foreign.

"Do you speak French?"

"I take French."

"That's what I mean! It's because of the contemporary school system that learning something doesn't equate to actually knowing it. I'm sure if I asked you if you understand the nature of forms, you'd slouch and mutter that you've taken trigonometry."

"No, I wouldn't."

"And why not?"

"I've never taken trigonometry."

He sat down next to me on the couch, slapped his knees, and bellied out wave after wave of wild delight. I made another move to leave, and he placed a restraining hand on my shoulder.

"I'm looking forward to seeing you again."

"Thanks for the water."

He followed me to the door.

"Happy New Year. I think this is going to be a good one."

"My mother used to tell me that odd years are times of evil."

He laughed once more.

"That's what every mother says, but this one is going to be different; I can feel it."

He smiled, but it looked like he was baring his teeth.

I didn't run until I had turned the corner.

ON THE SUBJECT OF WHY AYALE NEEDED A TV

My deliveries to these four continued up until December. I was always reluctant, but I never said no. For the first three recipients, there was just a hand slipped around the door, ready to receive my wares, and then there was Fiker, whose pronouncements gave me headaches that seemed to bleed into each other at every visit.

"Your punctuality is as delightful as your face on the rare occasions when you deign to smile."

"I hope you've read Bahru Zewde."

"Do you like me better now that you've seen my house?"

"Tell me you've read Bahru Zewde."

"Does my house remind you of your house?"

"I'll kill you if you haven't read Bahru Zewde."

"Will I ever see your house?"

"That was a joke! Are you crying again?"

Fiker's apartment contained a living room, a kitchen, and a window-less bedroom, with no bed. This last was the only space that bore evidence of human existence, since he never seemed to leave it. He had hung up a photograph of Mengistu Haile Mariam on one wall, a reminder against viciousness, and another of Haile Selassie, a reminder against foolishness. Cigarette packs ranging from Nyala to American Spirit lined the borders of his desk so that he could light one off the other without thinking. Magazines and newspapers covered the floor, except for the areas immediately in front of and behind his minute desk, which were taken up by dusty folding chairs. Two laptops and a desktop rested on the desk and the chair he wasn't sitting in, so that his infrequent guests were obliged to hold one of the three in their laps. Conversations were interrupted by urgent e-mails and phone calls to which he had to immediately respond and, afterward, recover from. I initially wondered if I was annoying him, but soon decided that this was the only way in which he could interact with the world: he was bored by less than four constant strands of thought, and he gave his full attention to each one, albeit in shifts. I couldn't imagine Elsie setting foot in the hovel, never mind living in it.

Each visit to his apartment became longer than the last. I don't quite know how to explain it, but I felt obliged to stay. Aside from frequently feeling ignored, when he did concentrate on me, it was like a high beam searing the residue off my eyeballs. These were unrelenting interrogations, and it wasn't so much that I didn't know the answers as that I didn't quite understand what the questions were really asking, why they were being asked, or if they even qualified as questions.

"Have you read James Baldwin?"

"Yes."

"Do you like him?"

"Yes."

"And you're a liberal?"

"What?"

"Are you a liberal because you actually believe in the liberal agenda, or are you a liberal because all young people think they should be liberal and so they support general 'liberalism' without truly comprehending what that means?"

"I . . . never said that I'm a liberal."

"So you're not a liberal?"

"I didn't say that, either."

"Would you define yourself as a progressive?"

"Yeah, sure."

"What are you progressing toward?"

"What?"

"What do you define as progress?"

"What?"

"Do you think that progress is happening all around you? Is it at a standstill?"

"I don't know!"

"Are you a political active?"

"What does that even mean? I would vote if I was the right age."

"Has your political unconscious awoken? Or does the beast remain unstirred?"

"I don't think I understand."

"Still sleeping. Pity."

He spoke to me in his elaborate English, reverting to Amharic only at the beginning and the end of my visits, so that it became the comforting entry point for transporting me into and out of English exigencies. It's too easy to say that he became my replacement for Ayale, so I won't.

Meanwhile, Ethiopians seemed to circle Americans, who seemed to circle Ethiopians, who seemed to circle Americans, ad infinitum, on my walks back and forth, to and from the bus stop, the convenience store, the laundromat. I wondered if it seemed to anyone else like our usually quiet street was now teeming with silent people, rigidly checking the time, window-shopping, craning their necks for the streetcar, debating between spicy wings and Subway. Perhaps this veneer of banality prevented everyone else from noticing how absurdly long it took them to complete each of these actions, the curious repetition of certain activities—how many times did one person have to check the price of a sub sandwich before crossing the street, crossing back, and checking again?—and the reappearance of certain people. My father told me he'd been feeling anxious.

"Anxious how?"

"I feel jumpy as soon as I leave my car, like there are too many people, but then there's never anyone there. I guess everyone's leaving the neighborhood. It feels deserted, doesn't it?"

"It just *seems* deserted."

"Have you noticed anything different?"

"No."

He gave me a look.

"You seem very sure of that."

"Why wouldn't I be?"

He backed off; if we had been wary of dispute before, it was now the booby trap we collectively strove to avoid, at all costs.

Despite my best efforts, I felt no safer; the rise in scrutiny made my world feel even more precarious, my identity ever more slippery, more problematic. I did my best to wrest circumstances into a more palatable form: I waved cheerfully at faces I saw more than twice, I asked my father about his childhood,

I hunted around the booth for postcards when I thought Ayale wasn't looking. It was all for naught. Only two people ever waved back and even then, only once, every other time stead-fastly looking past me no matter how vigorously I greeted them. Ayale caught me poking around and stopped letting me into the booth without him. Even the pleasure of learning more about my father was eclipsed by the news that our nearest Ethiopian neighbor had jumped from his sixth-floor window; his widow wept that he'd been a happy man, wept more when no one believed her.

I wasn't the only one feeling the effects of existential-bordering-on-cosmic disintegration. Ayale was having trouble understanding the dimensions of the world and how and where he fit into them. He would periodically pause to stare into space, coming out of his trance only with my insistent questioning about what he was doing, what was wrong, could I help.

"Would you say we're more northeast or northwest right now?"

"In relation to what?"

"These kinds of directions should never change."

"The river is west of us, right?"

"Never mind."

Not being able to deliver on what should have been a simple matter threw me into one of the black moods from which I found it more and more difficult to escape. Compounding it was the knowledge that upon leaving the lot every day, I had to contend with multiple pairs of eyeballs, all in the name of what was good for me, which left me raw-nerved. When my home-room teacher dropped a book, I screamed, then tried not to flinch as fifteen people's eyes locked onto me. I was so tired of being looked at.

Ayale began to participate in live online political forums

made up of middle-aged Ethiopian reactionaries. Soon, they were depending on him for ideas, jokes, advice. He had found a new landscape from which to pluck another flock of disciples.

He had also met a man known only by his Internet pseud-onym: Father. The two decided that joining forces would render them more useful for their cause, which, though never verbalized, was understood to be the same. We came to accept that between six P.M. on Friday and six A.M. on Monday, we wouldn't see Ayale. He hired a woman to leave covered plates of food outside his apartment door and became gaunt from the lack of seconds and thirds. He now went grocery shopping only when he had a craving for a specific food item and would purchase several jumbo-sized containers' worth of whatever he wanted, with the leftovers dumped onto us. These food drops were my introduction to pistachios, sun-dried tomatoes, Gru-yère, candied ginger.

"The boys and I were really busy this weekend" became a common greeting. Ayale called his online comrades "the boys," although I could never tell if this was an adoption of con-temporary parlance or an indication of his superiority. Nodding at Ayale had become our collective tic.

He developed the habit of dive-bombing into minute detail about obscure issues facing Ethiopian politicians, with abso-lutely no forewarning. The men would get restless, sneaking looks at their new BlackBerries, while my eyes got wider and wider, as if to catch something from the speechifying. At the moment of maximum inattention (he had a knack for gauging his audience), Ayale would ask the dreaded question: Do you understand? This was a lose-lose situation. If we said no, he would reexplain everything, slowly, on the brink of anger, until we felt that death might be preferable. If we said yes, he would ask us to elaborate, which we could never do sufficiently, not according to his standards. We would flounder until he pity-ingly saved us by fluidly synthesizing nineteen political points into a single unified argument. He would then ask us what the next step would be. We wouldn't have known that a next step could be possible. If we admitted this, he'd walk away. The more frequently these games occurred—because they were exactly that, play sessions wherein Ayale had all the fun, his questions labyrinths we couldn't escape—the more frequently I wanted to shove his body onto a landmine and hear the click before he exploded.

A few weeks after joining this new community, he told me that he'd be leaving for D.C.

"Just for a few days."

"Why?"

"The boys are having a conference. I'll be directing things while Father's away."

"Where's he going?"

"Israel."

I thought about this.

"Is he a real priest?"

He looked surprised by the question.

"Men of the cloth aren't always priests."

"What?"

He ignored me.

"Father made it clear that they couldn't possibly make it without me."

His casual tone hid none of his pride: he'd probably been hinting all along that they wouldn't know what to do without his guidance. I wondered if any of the boys hated Ayale.

When he returned from the trip, his skin was darker and radiated a new glow. I was afraid to get too close, sure that the thing pulsing throughout his body would burn me.

With the exception of Fiker, Ayale was tired of us. He wanted to be back with the boys. His responses were clipped. He would disappear with Fiker for hours, for the first time allowing the other attendants to ensure the effective carrying out of his system. Freak snowstorms at the end of September had already killed everything before the leaves could change; Thanksgiving, usually Ayale's favorite holiday, came and went without him noticing; I made halfhearted lists for my future and left them on the kitchen table, inextricable from the yellowed scraps where American names had been scrawled, messages for my father that I never gave him in time.

We were nearing Christmas when Ayale informed me that he was in dire need of a television. I asked him why and he said that he was falling behind, he wasn't getting information quickly enough; a TV was essential to joining the lineup of reality. I reminded him that he read the newspapers every day. He rolled his eyes (I had never seen him roll his eyes before) and said that he was tired of static news: if something were to happen in the afternoon, after all the newspapers had been printed, was he to depend on the half-baked theories of those around him to learn what was going on? Hadn't he come to America to escape propagandistic rumors? I explained that the two scenarios were nothing alike. He thundered that he would not go back into the dark of ignorance when the money and the technology to prevent it lay all around. I told him that it was just me, no need to go full Charlton-Heston-as-Moses. He laughed, and I grew foolhardy at this sign of approval.

"And besides, you could always just use your laptop. You'll have access to a million websites, television channels, all of it."

He scowled.

"I don't want to sit cowered over a small screen, trying to hear and see. A computer is a computer! A TV is a TV!"

He looked old, his skinny legs trembling in corduroys. Despite everything, I wanted to shield him from the truth that he desired on so large a scale. I began humming the theme from *The Sting*, my usual response to knowing that I didn't know a thing.

"Stop it."

Ayale was glaring at me with a ferocity that seemed unwarranted.

"That's a classic."

"What is it with you and that idiotic actor anyway?"

"Nothing."

"No really, tell me. I'd like to know."

His anger was frightening.

"He's made some incredible films."

"Name them."

"*All the President's Men.*"

"Dustin Hoffman. Next."

"*The Candidate.*"

"Bill Clinton did it better. What else?"

"*Ordinary People.*"

"He wasn't even in that!"

"But it's good, right?"

"You know what Robert Redford is? A white man whose success is due entirely to being a white man. And you know the worst thing about him? He actually finds himself *profound*. He fancies himself an *activist*. He must burst into tears sometimes, just *thinking* about how noble he is."

"My mother loved him."

He snorted.

"Your mother loved a lot of things that didn't do her any good."

I looked at him, he looked back, and I thought I could see fright in his eyes.

"You know my mother."

"No."

"Then why did you say that."

Neither of us raised our voices; neither of us dared.

"I don't know."

"Bullshit."

"Don't swear."

"How do you know her?"

"The real question is, how *could* I know her?"

"Tell me."

"Isn't it obvious that someone who married your father probably doesn't have the best judgment? Don't you think that's a fair assessment of character?"

He was recovering now.

"You don't know my father."

He threw up his hands.

"I sometimes think I don't know you, so who's to say?"

I left him there, with something that tasted like vomit making it difficult for me to swallow.

Ayale would later buy a television from the back of a man's truck. I've always wondered why it took him so long. I wonder if he was afraid of what he might see.

On the Subject of Love

It was on Christmas Eve, not a creature stirring, not even a mouse, that an apartment building in "Best Place to Raise Your Kids" Malden was torched. Twenty-five people stumbled out of bed, twenty-five people tried to reassemble the universe, twenty-five people ran toward exits that seemed farther away than yesterday, twenty-four people died in various attitudes of grotesque suffocation. The only survivor was seven years old and immediately christened "a miracle." Of the twenty-four, twenty-three were Ethiopian. This had been a well-known gathering place for the people of the Horn, thanks to the first-floor community rooms that could be rented out for free, provided you knew a tenant. Many a wedding, baptism, birthday party, and funeral sitting had been stationed here, with celebrations often overflowing into the surrounding lot—whose evening "residents only" policy caused drunken merrymakers to scramble—and first kisses being gingerly planted in the ill-lit park in the back, the building's glass-walled rooms looking out on these unhappy couples of the future.

For the first time, the killings attracted attention beyond the Ethiopian clusters. This was front-page news, this was the-war-at-home, this was round-the-clock investigation, this was could-be-terrorists, this was is-our-immigration-policy-flawed, this was American-Dream-under-attack. As the victims' names were released, there came a flood of articles, probing the coincidence of so many from the same ethnic group being burned alive. Maps of Africa with Ethiopia indicated via helpful circles and arrows were displayed next to these texts, to provide context, but also establishing a subtext that the authors had perhaps not intended. I was asked in class to explain my views and met with bafflement when I couldn't present satisfactory or reassuring interpretations. Some of my classmates were even more perplexed by the fact that I wasn't related to any of the victims. Ethiopia's seventy-three million inhabitants didn't appear to be adequate justification for my grievous lack of blood relation, but the questions died down after the *Herald* unleashed a five-page spread headlined, "Was It Their Fault?"

Damning materials found on-site proved arson, but by whom and for what purpose was the shimmering mystery.

My father and I didn't leave the house for the rest of my school vacation. There was no discussion of the matter. He called in sick for the first time since I'd known him, and our only interaction with the outside world came with the Chinese delivery people, who, as fellow strangers to America, soothed us. We watched movies, read books, and finally, truly spoke to each other. It was slow at first, brief observations and the like, but this soon blossomed into sometimes hours-long conversations.

These were not biographical in nature; we had both lost interest in childhood anecdotes. Instead, we wanted to know what the other thought about politics, the upstairs neighbors, eighties sitcoms, white people. I finally understood that fundamentally, my father neither liked nor enjoyed nor treasured children. Beyond my being his daughter, there wasn't much about me that interested him until he could relate to me in the only way he knew how: as a friend.

Ayale didn't call. We watched TV, mocking nightly news programs' usual patterns of human interest stories combined with inflammatory language, and still, Ayale did not call. He was the one subject I actively avoided with my father, and I appreciated that he didn't broach it, either. My sadness overwhelmed me, and for the first time, when I cried, I didn't shut myself in my room, and he didn't leave to get cigarettes.

Returning to school, I sensed the shift on the street. There were eyes everywhere, that hadn't changed, but they were different ones. There were no visible bodies to attach them to like before. There were only my neighbors and the usual denizens of the area, but the mass had tripled nonetheless, and the thickness of the air made it hard to breathe. The weight was too great to be sustained; I knew that the cataclysm was imminent.

It was when I was taking my usual route home that the summons came, delivered by a disciple pretending to be lost: "Come by the lot, no time to waste." When I arrived, I saw that the weight I sensed on my street had lodged itself inside Ayale, making his skin swollen, his eyes bulging, his body more capable of hurt. He didn't bear the usual signs of his anger, but there could be no doubt that whatever he was feeling was a kissing cousin to it.

"Are you all right?"

I almost laughed.

"It took you a while to ask."

He wasn't paying attention.

"I don't think it's a good idea for you to stay here."

His eyes kept ticking over to the right and left before alighting on my face and then repeating the movement.

"You asked me to come."

He seemed taken aback until he remembered. I felt such tenderness for his confusion: at last, I could relate.

"It's terrible, what happened," he whispered.

"It is."

We waited.

"What are you doing tomorrow?"

"I don't think—"

"I'll pay you double! And it's safe."

I took a step back.

"I didn't think it wasn't safe."

"Well, because it is."

"So why did you say that?"

"Just . . . these are uncertain times."

The silence stretched forward, interminable, until for reasons still unknown (although I have a few educated guesses), I nodded yes.

"You'll only have an hour, and you have to be here at five in the morning."

"I can't get a bus at five! Can you pick me up?"

He was practically pleading.

"If I could, I'd do it myself. This is the last time, I promise. And it's extremely important."

Despite myself, I laughed.

"Relatives from Ethiopia, huh?"

He tried to smile back.

"Only the best for my customers."

"I'll figure it out," I called over my shoulder as I left.

I never set foot in the lot again.

This was to be my last year in Boston. I had gotten into a college farther north, one that had agreed to subsidize me, provided I maintained a certain average, wrote annual thank-you notes to my coma-bound patrons, and didn't cause any trouble. (The Ethnic Students Admissions student volunteer gently advised that I stay away from unsavory associations like the African-American House, the tennis team, the Liberal Party, the Conservative Party.) I didn't quite believe I was leaving. Whenever I imagined abandoning this city of color-coded trains, sadistic bus drivers, contaminated rivers, and nasality, I would become terrified and then furious at myself for not embracing a good thing. College was my means of escape. There would always be more education to excuse my pulling away forever.

On that bus ride home, I began feeling nostalgic about Ayale. I would say it was as if I knew that our time together was coming to an end, but I've never been the kind of person who knows anything soon enough to make a difference. I tried to remind myself that he was a dangerous man to whom I had become far too attached. I would forget him once I was nestled in the blissful ignorance of too little sleep and too much alcohol. Thanks to talk shows, I knew that institutions of higher learning were knee-deep in the stuff and that if I wasn't careful, I would be alcohol poisoned by my second week. I looked forward to this new way of forgetting.

But until then, I couldn't let go of the feeling that everything was on the brink of collapse, that I'd soon find myself smothered by the debris. I changed buses and, in what felt like too little time to prepare for truth, was standing in front of Fiker's building. I dove in as soon as he opened the door, afraid of what was lying in wait, outside and inside.

"What's really in the boxes? Has Ayale been lying this *whole* time? And, honestly, why me? Of all the people, ever, why *me*?"

He led me to my usual chair. It was taking him so long to respond that I assumed he wouldn't but also couldn't think of anything to say in this breach of not knowing. He straightened, as if having arrived at a decision.

"It's a bit hard to explain."

I had never known Fiker to find anything even slightly difficult to explain.

"Because this is actually too complicated a plot? Or because you don't think I should know?"

"Ah, plot. Story, scheme, parcel of land, all three: which definition were you leaning toward?"

"It's just a word."

"That's too easy."

"Nothing is *too* easy."

"I'm just trying to help you understand—"

"Let's skip to the part of the movie where I'm bleeding and tied up and you're the guy who tells me everything I should have known for the first half, except that I was too good-looking and cocky to notice."

"As much as I don't want to feed into any James Bond complexes, I take your point."

Fiker reached for the laptop I'd been jiggling around with my knees and started typing with a speed that was insulting. Once finished, he reread his message, tapped a few other keys, pushed the laptop toward me, and then leaned back in his chair.

"How long have you known Ayale?"

"Fairly long."

"In human time?"

"About two years."

"Not long at all."

"For me that's long."

"I forget you're very young."

A pause, a cigarette, an appraisal before he continued.

"I shall take the liberty of assuming that Ayale hasn't shared the particulars of his vision with you, namely because it took a bit of force on my part to be taken into his version of confidence."

"What vision?"

"He's creating a country. One of his very own."

"What?"

"A nation with cultural authenticity from Ethiopia and the latest in technology, medicine, and entertainment from America. First and third worlds coming together in a marriage of equals."

I took a breath and tried to find a way to make any of this seem real or right.

"But how do you even get a new country? Do you go to . . . a land store?"

"That's ridiculous."

"*That's* ridiculous?"

"The only way to acquire anything on the higher end of valuable is through definitive action."

"Who would be the recipient of this . . . definitive action?"

"There are a few targets."

"Explain."

My jaw hurt, and I was getting a headache.

"You may not know this, but there's contested land between Somalia and Ethiopia. It's the usual game: Ethiopia claims divine right, Somalia puts its finger on its nose—"

"Why would Somalia do that?"

"—and says that Ethiopia's a bully, taking land by night and saying it was there by day, etcetera. So there are battles. One- or two-day skirmishes during the lean years, to keep up morale. Ethiopia says the inhabitants of the area consider themselves Ethiopians. Somalia scorns the notion. No one knows what the inhabitants say, because they're never asked."

"Okay. I'm following you, I really am, I just have no idea how you take over a piece of land that two whole countries can't settle between themselves."

"No one's *taking over*. Ayale became interested for personal reasons: a good friend died while trying to fight his way out."

I had to remind myself to breathe.

"I didn't know."

"Most people don't. But he couldn't let it go without trying to do something. And he decided that the only thing he *could* do, that would actually make a difference, was to join those caught in the middle: fight against their oppressors, channel all the supplies and money at his disposal toward their cause, do everything in his power to make sure they won their war of independence."

"But then . . . they'll be independent. I thought he wanted his own country?"

Fiker looked uncomfortable.

"It seems more than likely that in return for his aid, Ayale can expect to receive recognition."

I thought about this.

"You mean that he wants first shot at running the place."

"It only seems fair."

"Does it?"

"Unusually, I have no desire to discuss the semantics of morality with you, especially the morality of another."

"You're involved in this?"

He bowed in what I believe was meant to be a gesture of humility.

"How?"

"I have been directing our people who are already in situ: we have messengers going door to door, disseminating Ayale's message, garnering support. Others are making themselves indispensable through their skills and participation in communal life. The inhabitants see them as one of their own. I'll admit that they were hesitant about independence before, even though it was clearly their best option. But they falter no longer. We're winning them over with respect, with brotherhood."

"With love."

"Precisely."

I looked at a stain on his desk.

"Is Fiker your real name?"

I didn't look up until I was sure he was done laughing.

"You weren't part of this originally. You said he didn't want to tell you anything."

"Your point?"

"Why did he keep it from you? How did you get him to tell you?"

"Next question."

I sighed.

"The boxes?"

"We have scouts in Somalia and Ethiopia, collecting information from government assemblies, determining where everyone stands on the land. You've been delivering their reports."

The last word triggered something painful.

"Are the people who died part of this?"

My heart was trying to beat its way out of my chest. I put a hand there as feeble defense, as he reached across and took my other hand.

"Neither Ayale nor I laid a finger on anyone." He patted my hand before releasing it. "Not one finger. Remember that."

I was torn between doubt and profound relief.

"Why is he so obsessed with this online stuff?"

I tried to wipe off where Fiker had touched me without his noticing. He rubbed his eyes.

"He needs a base in the States. Father helps him guide forum discussions."

"And . . . Washington, D.C., is . . ."

He nodded.

"Meetings where he pitches the idea of a different kind of homeland." He noted my confusion. "He needs talented people to settle there once everything is ready. Preferably young, no families, a thirst for adventure. With what they have to offer, he'd have a greater chance of creating something sustainable on the first go-round. Ayale's been doing quite well. It helps that Father has such an extensive network there."

"Who's Father?"

He leaned back far enough that his eyes were fixed on the ceiling.

"Do you remember a little monk, in a little house, on a little street?"

I sprang up and began to pace as much as the confines of the room would allow.

"And do you remember a little island he told you about? A little island called—"

"Get to the point."

He chuckled.

"That little island on the back of the postcard is Ayale's test run. He needs investors for his plan, and they need proof. He's set up, on a small scale, what he believes to be the ideal structure for our new nation; if it keeps going well, they'll chip in, and he can move forward with greater speed, and even more firepower."

He smiled the widest of his questionable dental productions.

"Why did Father talk to us?"

"He was recruiting in Boston before he went to D.C." Fiker rolled his eyes. "I challenge you to find another city with more small-minded, unimaginative specimens of our people. Father talked to every single Ethiopian here, trying to find *anyone* who might be suitable for our island community. He liked you, especially your father, but he had a feeling you wouldn't be interested."

"Why didn't we hear about him from other people?"

He looked startled.

"Since when do either of you *ever* speak to other people?"

I pressed on.

"Fine, you've got people, maybe investors, but you need money to . . . of course."

"The lots. Exactly."

"But he has to pay off so many people. There's no way that he could have enough."

"Are you sure?"

"I'm not sure about anything! But he said he barely has enough to pay his own bills."

"Is that so?"

"Jesus, if you don't agree, just say it. You don't have to humor me."

"I respect the fact that you love Ayale"—he raised his hand to fend off my protests, waited until I'd subsided—"and that you want him to be as much in the right as possible. But we're talking about a man who picks and chooses the truths he tells people, based on what he thinks he can squeeze out of them. That being said, I *do* think he's been more forthright with you than he's been with most, and I'm not saying that to *humor* you, I'm saying it because I think it's true. Nonetheless, you can't change someone's nature, especially one like Ayale's."

"You keep saying 'he,' not 'we.' Are you part of this or are you not?"

"Irrelevant."

"You grew up together, didn't you?"

"Our mothers knew each other."

"You must love each other very much."

He snorted.

"You're forgetting just how much over the limit Ayale can go. Yes, it's been getting harder to hide, and yes, he's had to add a few people to the payroll, but he's bringing in so much that a good week might yield as much as ten thousand dollars."

"Fuck me."

"Remember that before you and Ayale met, he'd already been working for a decade, and it only took him six months to realize that there was a better way of doing things. Factor in also that the other parking lots are not separate entities."

"Excuse me?"

"Quite a few of our men owe Ayale favors—surely you've noticed that yourself. There have been, on occasion, weaker men who in their weaker moments took a bit from the till and panicked. He gave them money, won over their bosses, then persuaded them that instead of paying him back or offering their firstborn, they should give him a very low percentage of their salary. He would put it toward a larger investment, which he would supervise. They were only too happy to comply, bowled over by a man who wanted a favor that was ultimately a favor to them. Ayale did indeed invest their money wisely, and that's a hefty nest egg in and of itself. Not to mention the taxi."

"What taxi?"

I had laid my head down on my arms and was speaking directly into his desk.

"Actually, there are three of them."

"Of course there are. Who gets less than three these days?"

"He leases them out, with his own drivers at the wheel, and takes a cut of whatever they earn, so they make damn sure to get the largest tips they can."

"But with all the things he pays for, how does he still have enough for his . . . cause?"

"You're looking at the short term. Ayale is all about the big picture. The only small details he focuses on are the ones that actually make a difference."

"And me? Do *I* make a difference? What is he planning on doing about *me*?"

I was speaking so quickly that my tongue kept getting in the way of my language. He offered me a Gauloises.

"No matter what you think about the man, at the end of the day, he's helping a nation gain its rightful sovereignty. In return, he'd like a say in how it's run. Sure, there are illegal numbers of cars parked here and there, but can't you see how freedom trounces any law?"

"He asked me to go to the lot for a delivery."

"When?"

"Tomorrow morning."

"Will you go?"

"Will I be safe?"

He laughed.

"You've never been safe."

A coldness was spreading through my body.

"Why am I making deliveries to you four, specifically? Who *exactly* are you?"

"See you tomorrow."

"Is the delivery for you? I thought you said I wasn't safe?"

"But you've always known that. Will you start to disappoint now?"

I looked at him, hunched over and filthy. He wouldn't blink if I was the next one in the papers. Just so long as he got a piece of this country. I didn't turn when he said my name.

Ayale never called again, not even when I didn't show up for my promised delivery, and the volume of unseen onlookers seemed to increase by the minute. In the absence of anyone else, I clung to my father. He finally offered to go to the lot to speak to Ayale himself, but I begged him not to, terrified of what might happen to him. I hadn't told him about what I'd learned, but I didn't have to: there was something new and putrid stinking up our existence.

I sometimes try to believe that the decision to abandon me was meant as a service; rather than put me through the torture of having to decide between him and moral justice—and, frankly, my own mortality—Ayale made the choice for me. He tried to spare me. At other times, I see it as the selfish act it was, the vanishing of a man who no longer needed me to bolster what had taken him so long to build. In any case, the outcome remains the same: none of us got what we wanted.

On the Subject of
How Everyone Found Out and
Didn't Like It

I had never been called out of class before. There had never been a need to notify me of a relative's death or a forgotten doctor's appointment. I'd seen the inside of the principal's office only when I was sent by teachers to pick up their mail or ask the secretaries if the Halloween party would cut into class time. Nonetheless, I hadn't forgotten the grade school awe that accompanied the PA crackling to life and calling Natalie Fergus or Michael Mayer to the office. The teacher could say nothing to them, not even what the homework would be, if they didn't wish to stop and listen. I dreamt of owning this impenetrable cloak.

When the student monitor came into my literature class, we were discussing *Crime and Punishment* and eating Munchkins.

I had stuffed an entire chocolate glazed into my mouth to conceal the fact that I'd taken the last one. When I was called to the front, I swallowed too quickly and arrived at Ms. Diamond's desk in a mess of crumbs and coughing. As I stood there dying, she informed me that I was to go to the guidance counselors' office. I was intrigued. I'd seen my guidance counselor just once; after recounting her sons' rehab misadventures, she had mentioned that only problem students bothered their counselors and so she didn't anticipate seeing me again before graduation. I took the hint.

I climbed the stairs to the fourth floor because elevator keys were given only to the handicapped kids, who had no other joy in their half-mobile lives. Instead of my counselor, it was the headmaster who greeted me. She wore skirt-and-blazer sets with white athletic sneakers and support hose, and camouflaged her Boston accent with inflections she believed aristocratic. I felt manipulated into liking her because she was the school's first female headmaster.

On this occasion however, I was distracted by the two police officers who stood behind her. I tried to meet their eyes as I took a seat in front of her desk, but I was having trouble focusing.

"How are things, dear?"

The headmaster said "dear" only when she was trying to care, which meant that you might need her care, which meant that you were royally fucked.

"Good."

"Any trouble at home?"

"No."

"I would ask about trouble at school, but we all know that's not an issue!"

She laughed heartily, and the officers did their best to join in.

The man who owned the truck was talking about Haiti, and he was talking about Haiti to talk about freedom, and he was talking about that because, man, if you didn't have freedom, and you didn't have Haiti, what the fuck *did* you have?

"Public order."

The man looked uncertain, but then whooped and slapped Ayale on the back; Ayale tried not to flinch as cars flew past their position by the parked truck.

"I bet they called you Lion in school."

Ayale was uncertain as to why this nickname would have been appropriate.

"So you're telling me that a color television is not actually necessary?"

"All I'm saying is, if you want it in color, why not just go live some real life?"

The man's shoulders shook with the effort and pleasure of laughing.

"But you're advising me to buy a black-and-white television set?"

"Television is art, right? *Art* is art, right? So you want something that makes it obvious, from the very beginning, that this is art, *straight up*, this isn't something that might play you by *pretending* that it's a *substitute* for your *reality*. You feel me?"

The man's habit of emphasizing key words proved unhelpful for identifying what the key words actually were.

"Do you not have any color televisions?"

"Of *course* I do! What century are we living in? Huh? Brother? Ma'am, can you tell me what century we're living in? Brother don't even know!"

THE PARKING LOT ATTENDANT   181

The woman who had been accosted in the man's pageantry of mock confusion quickly veered away, which made him double over, giggling.

"What do you usually do after school?"

This came from Officer Carroll, who had just finished telling me how his daughter and I had gone to the same elementary school; he remembered seeing my face in the schoolyard.

"Homework, home."

"Any extracurriculahs?"

"I help with theater."

"That's great! That's fantastic! What kind of theatah? What do you do?"

The headmaster jumped in, too excited to let this opportunity pass.

"She's involved with the school's Shakespeare group—they act out scenes from the Shakespeare for our English classes. I think we saw you last as Hamlet?"

I had never played anything before, but I nodded because I had a feeling that my being Hamlet would make things easier on everyone, especially me. Indeed, after my affirmation, the room's atmosphere did lighten a bit.

"Wow, what an honah. What else do you like to do?"

"I read."

Officer Carroll nodded knowledgeably, as if he had heard of this obscure pastime.

"That's really good, sweethaht. Who's ya favorite authah?"

"I don't know."

"That's okay!"

He smiled encouragingly.

"Why don't we stick to the questions we wrote down," whispered the other officer, Downing, who had apparently dispensed with the need for blinking.

"Totally, Rob, totally. Okay, sweethaht, now that we gota bettah idea of where *yar* coming from and what *youah* like to do, we gotta ask you about something *specific*. Is that okay with you?"

"Sure."

"Are you familiar with a person named Ayale?"

"You don't say it like the school, there's an accent, but yes, I know him."

"Are you related?"

"No."

"Would you say that yar friends with him?"

"That depends."

"You'd do better to answer their questions," whispered the headmaster.

"I'm trying," I whispered back.

"Get to the end," whispered Officer Downing.

"I'm *trying*," said Officer Carroll.

Officer Downing took over.

"When you're not acting or reading, do you go to the parking lot near S——?"

"Sometimes."

"Ayale works there."

"I know."

"You're there quite often, it seems. Almost every day."

"Okay."

"Is there a reason why a young girl like you is so fascinated by a parking lot?"

"I like cars."

They laughed.

"Why not switch it up sometimes? Try a showroom?"

"I can do my homework there. It's nice to meet so many different people. And my family's Ethiopian, so it helps me be more active in the community."

This seemed to be what Officer Downing had been waiting for.

"Isn't it funny that all of the attendants are Ethiopian? I mean, don't get me wrong, I *love* your food, but doesn't it strike you as slightly *weird* that there are so many Ethiopians working there, hanging out there, presumably for the same reason, to be a part of the *community*?"

"Why weird? Italians own everything in the North End and no one seems to care."

"Let me make it clear that community building among minority populations is something that we encourage and foster. But there's a difference between a community and a gang."

"I am *not* part of a gang."

"How well do you know Ayale?"

"Not that well."

"Even though you see him every day? Even though you go out with him on weekend late nights? Even though you've been carrying packages for him for over a year?"

This was when I vomited colored sugar on the floor and we had to take a break to clean up.

⸻

"I'll give it to you for a thousand."

"You must be joking."

"It's a color television! It's almost a flatscreen!"

"There's no such thing as 'almost,' and it's only flat there because someone punched it in."

"Less than that and I might as well just give it to you for free."

"So give it to me for free."

"You funny man, you real funny."

"I'll take it for a hundred dollars."

"Get the fuck out of my face."

"What I'm offering you is highway robbery."

"Good-bye."

"There's no way that this will get you anything more than a hundred."

"You're insulting me now. You really are. I've never been so insulted in my life."

"An intelligent man would take the hundred and kiss my feet for it, too."

"An intelligent man can kiss my ass."

"Come on, come on, let's talk, don't act like that."

"How can I help it? When you insult me, when you pretend you're giving me a gift and you're just stealing my shit?"

"I can't give you a thousand."

"If you give me seven hundred, we can shake hands and part like brothers."

"I don't need any more brothers. One-fifty."

"Are you out of your mind?"

"I'm trying to meet you halfway."

"I should have just moved back to Haiti if this is the way it's gonna be here."

"Maybe."

"Man, do you *know* where you are?"

"Welcome to America."

"We need to tell you something."

I was back in my seat, mortified. The headmaster had tactfully pushed my chair farther away.

THE PARKING LOT ATTENDANT   185

"The FBI is in on everything."

"What are you talking about?"

"This is a matter of national security."

"Wait, are you serious?"

"We think you're involved in something that you don't understand the first thing about."

"I do! I understand everything!"

Officer Downing braved my uncertain stomach and knelt beside me.

"You need to be honest with us."

Ayale and the man settled on four hundred. The man chuckled as he counted out the crisp bills.

"She knows you like the back of her hand, man."

Ayale looked at him.

"She?"

"Yeah, man, she knew you'd go up to four hundred. That woman is nobody's fool, that's for damn sure." He took in Ayale's expression. "What's wrong, brother?"

At that moment, four police cars zoomed into formation around the truck, a single police officer jumping out of each vehicle. One walked up to Ayale, smiling, apologizing for the fact that they had to take him in for some questions. The television man didn't linger; he jumped into his truck, but before racing off, stuck his head out the glassless window.

"She said to tell you: 'I told you I'd do it better.' "

Ayale had to laugh, even if all of it just made him want to cry.

"When was Ayale born?"

"I don't know."

"Come on, the year."

"I don't know."

"You're lying."

"I really don't know."

"The date on his passport says 1954."

"That's a mistake."

"So you *do* know when he was born?"

"No."

"How did you meet him?"

"By accident."

"Any prior connections?"

"Shared ethnic background."

"Were you ever lovers?"

"That's disgusting."

"Was your relationship purely personal or did it also encompass business matters?"

"No."

"You *gotta* be more *specific*," Officer Carroll jumped in. The intensity of the situation was getting to him.

"I'm a student. What kind of business connections could we possibly have?"

"You were acting as a messenger."

"That doesn't make any sense. I've always been present for my classes."

"She's not lying," said the headmaster to no one in particular.

"You went in the afternoon."

"This is ridiculous."

"False bravado will get you nowhere, my dear."

"It's gotten me this far."

"Do you know where they are? The people on your route?"

"What route? What people? No?"

"All of them, without exception, are missing."

"I can't help you. I don't know where they are."

"Are you aware of a land transaction that Ayale and his collaborators are connected to?"

I was caught off guard.

"No?"

Still kneeling, Officer Downing put his face so close to mine that I could have counted pores if I'd been so inclined.

"What would you say if I told you that Ayale is a known agitator who has spent his years in the U.S. inciting unrest, instigating riots, only to slip across the border at the last moment? What if I told you that he's pushing for a war against both Ethiopia and Somalia, supposedly on behalf of a people who are actually being slaughtered if they so much as breathe dissent against him? That the death toll is staggering?"

He was lying. He was exaggerating to drag something out of me. I had to stay strong.

"I'd say you've been watching too many movies."

He nodded slowly.

"I'm sure you're aware of the murders, all Ethiopian, all brutal?"

"I'm aware."

"Are you also aware that all of them, without exception, were linked to the most influential members of the Somalian and Ethiopian Parliaments, in ways that those members wished to keep concealed? Are you aware of just how close Ayale is to colonizing a country, becoming a dictator?"

If I looked at the floor, it was easier not to cry. I didn't respond. He waited a beat.

"We know you helped him kill them."

My head flew up.

"What are you talking about?! I'm seventeen! The way they were killed, I couldn't have done it!"

Officer Downing contemplated his nails for a moment. He turned toward Officer Carroll. "Did we release any details regarding the murders?"

"Nope."

Officer Carroll was beginning to look more and more like his bitch daughter.

"We're going to have to take you in. If the headmaster doesn't mind?"

She bowed her head.

As we walked out (the bell had rung for the end of fourth period; some kids were rushing to lunch, others to class; I heard someone say that they'd found weed in my locker), we passed the open door of a girls' bathroom. I turned and saw in the cracked mirror that an enormous smear of chocolate flavoring encrusted the left side of my mouth. Despite everything, I was still me.

Ayale didn't waste time: upon arrival at the station, he sat before the three officers into whose care he'd been roughly shoved and quietly explained what his rights were, how he understood that perhaps they were not aware of just how furiously they'd trampled all over them, and that the only way to rectify this situation—which was hanging by a thread, he thought they ought to know—was to either immediately release him on some kind of probationary status or allow him to call his lawyer, wait for his lawyer, and discuss the situation with his lawyer. Then, and only then, would he be able to answer questions. Since this consultation period was bound to take no less than forty-eight hours, it was imperative that they either provide accommodation or release him into his lawyer's care, and also, he'd had neither breakfast nor lunch and would appreciate a sandwich, for which, of course, he would pay, just as soon as they returned his wallet. Coffee would also be wonderful.

Temporary exit procedures can take no time at all, with the right people driving them forward. Ayale lunched at South Street Diner, where he kept looking over his shoulder and the unfamiliar day staff gave him funny looks, as if they could smell the stench of dubious authority.

I was taken to another precinct, where one of the secretaries gave me a white foam cup filled to the brim with Lipton tea, which I had trouble keeping steady. I was put into the care of a man and a woman, the former with red hair, the latter with none; her head sparkled and looked as though olive oil had been rubbed into its small-pored surface.

"Would you consider Ayale a good man?" she asked.

"Excuse me?"

"Would you say that he has the best interests of everyone in mind, be it himself, you, his friends, his family, society?"

"Yes."

"What makes you think that?"

"It's just what I think."

"Can you elaborate?"

"No."

"Did you talk about the murders with him?"

"A little bit."

"What did you say to each other?"

"That it was really sad."

"What else?"

"That was it."

"What's your general opinion of him?"

I couldn't just believe them without speaking to Ayale first.

No matter how compelling the evidence, no matter how probable their theories—and what did it mean if I knew someone who seemed *likely* to kill, to subjugate?—I couldn't just take the word of the enemy. Even if I still didn't understand who the enemy was.

"I have a lot of respect for him."

"Do you respect his engineering of an uprising on another continent?"

"No comment."

"Because you don't know?"

"Yes."

"Or because you don't want to?"

"Yes."

"Does it bother you that the men who were supposed to be protecting you would have killed you if it meant saving themselves, saving him? That he, quite frankly, didn't care about you at all?"

"I don't know what you're talking about."

Words were difficult to form, what with the snot and tears that were clogging my every facial orifice.

"Let's take a break."

Word spread fast as to my whereabouts. When Ayale got wind of what was going on, he called up some contacts and had them keep a lookout. Upon leaving that night, exhausted, having promised to return in the morning, I found a taxi waiting at the curb. I didn't question its origin and fell asleep in the back, waking up only when the driver gently shook me.

"Oh hi . . . where are we?"

He helped me out; one of my legs had fallen asleep.

"Sixth floor, second door on your right."

I had trouble getting my bearings. I was standing by one of the entrances to what I now saw was an enormous apartment complex. It reminded me in structure and style of the one that had been set ablaze, and when I faltered, he gently pushed me forward.

"Can't you just tell me where I am?"

"I'm so sorry. Take care."

I watched, confused, as he ran into his car, honked three times, and peeled away. Having nothing else to do, I followed his instructions.

When I arrived at the door in question, it swung open and a hand pulled me inside, none too gently. The apartment seemed lit with the sole agenda of creating as many pockets of darkness as possible. There were lamps everywhere, but most were covered with scarves, so that all illumination was filtered in such a way that everyone and everything looked sprayed with a light smattering of grime. The woman who led me inside was my height, and when she turned, I saw that she was somewhere in her mid-twenties.

After sitting me down on a couch, she returned a few minutes later with a tray of soft drinks, the bottles laid out flat like the servants do it in Ethiopia, and a basket of salted peanuts, because *kolo* is hard to find. Next was a pot of hot coffee, and when I bolted upright from sleep, Ayale was sitting across from me, tranquilly sipping from my cold mug.

"Why don't you ever put in sugar?"

"You!"

He looked up sharply.

"What?"

It was taking my brain too long to wake up, and now he had my coffee.

"I was at the police station."

"Oh?"

"It was horrible."

"What did you tell them?"

"Nothing."

"Tell me exactly what you told them."

"Why don't you tell me what's going on first?"

He began to pace the room.

"As I understand it, at around the same time that you were taken, I was brought before the police and was allowed to leave after about thirty minutes. For various reasons, it took me four hours to get home, where my front door had been kicked in. Inside, all electronics had been removed, highly sensitive papers were missing, others were scattered. Furniture was scuffed. For some mysterious reason, all forms of soap had been confiscated."

"That's not what I meant."

"I went straight back to the police, to the exact station where I had been apprehended."

"What?"

I had never heard anything more moronic. Ayale nodded, grimly enjoying how, once again, I wasn't nearly agile enough to follow the leaps and bounds of his thinking.

"I wanted them to see me as a genuine victim, innocent enough to view the police as a force of good. It didn't escape me that it had to be one of theirs who had so thoroughly explored my home, don't worry."

"So?" My vocabulary was gone.

"After filling out some forms, I was waylaid and told that new information directly implicated me. When asked about sources, proof, of course they weren't at liberty to say. I'd expected as much."

"They know everything," I said quietly.

THE PARKING LOT ATTENDANT   193

He sat down.

"I know they do. Tell me what you said. I need to evaluate the extent of the damage."

This took hours. I could barely get through half a dozen sentences without him interrupting and asking me to clarify a detail or go back over a sequence of events that he hadn't quite understood. I spoke on automatic, too tired to be frightened, and when I'd finished, the layer of grime had been replaced by an ashy glow, courtesy of the just rising sun. The girl reappeared with coffee and toast. Ayale thanked her kindly, and I eked out a smile that she didn't return. He reached for a piece, and the scraping of the butter knife echoed in this room that persisted in resisting natural light. It was only after finishing his first slice that he spoke.

"I'll get someone to drive you home."

"Tell me."

"Tell you what?"

"Is it true? Were they lying?"

He finished a second slice before he spoke.

"I'll be leaving tonight."

"You said not for another year!"

I almost felt betrayed; what a joke.

"Once you start losing, it's hard to get out of that pattern. Remember that."

Everyone's always telling me to remember things that I'd rather forget.

"Where will you go?"

"I think you know."

I looked at him for a moment.

"Would you change anything?"

He guffawed.

"You've always asked the wrong questions. There are people

who help you and people who hurt you. You keep the former until they become the latter and hope that you never hurt the former. I made a mistake. That's the only change that matters now."

The girl returned and waited by the door until I rose and walked toward her. When I had passed through the doorway, I turned back, perhaps for a last glimpse or plea, but she blocked my view, and so there was nothing for it but to keep moving, from the complex to the taxi, from the taxi to my door, from my door to my father, from him to the explanations about where I'd been, what was wrong, why were there so many police officers on our street, *what was wrong*, for God's sake.

As he shouted, I thought back to a lifetime ago, when I'd first met Ayale; I'd been so arrogant, so sure I was something special because I had one or two quips up my sleeve. He'd made a mistake when he'd kept me, perhaps the first of his life. I had failed him. I was a failure. It didn't occur to me that perhaps it was he who had failed me.

My father was crying, Ayale was leaving, and I was failing. We were all accounted for now.

ON THE SUBJECT OF
HOW IT ENDED THERE BEFORE WE
CAME TO HERE

The fallout was swift in that there were no ostensible signs of one. Investigations into the murders continued, while the murders themselves didn't. No valid connection between them and Ayale has yet to be publicly announced, while the Ethiopian rumor mill remains split on the subject.

My father received a garbled account that featured parking lots in light doses, Ayale as a hapless victim of a blurry foe, and the police as the truly regrettable by-product of it all. I was too afraid to walk at my graduation and received my diploma in the mail. When I showed it to my father, he gazed at the Latin before handing it back.

"It'll be good for you to go away. Meet new people."

I had already made my decision.

"I'm not going to college. I'm sorry. I just can't yet."

He stayed silent, searching for his lighter, finding a box of matches underneath the couch.

"I'll pay you back the deposit. I'll get a job. But I can't do it."

He lit his cigarette.

"I'll make you a deal."

"What's the deal?"

I was wary of anything that resembled a covenant.

"Defer your status."

"And do what?"

"I'll think of something."

A month later, he told me that we were going to B——, to soak up a new environment, take part in a better adventure. I refused. When asked why, I said only that I couldn't. When asked if I had a better plan, I assured him that any plan was better than going to B——. He gently explained that it was all arranged and that if we stayed in Boston, he had it on good authority that neither of us would be safe. I even more gently replied that he had no idea what he was talking about, especially in terms of what was safe. He leaned against the counter by the sink, arms crossed.

"I know that *he's* involved with B——. I don't know how or why, nor do I want to, and I hope you don't, either, because from the little I know, it sounds like a mess. I don't want you to worry about that. We'll be fine. Anyway, you haven't done anything wrong." When I opened my mouth to protest, he shook his head. "You've done nothing wrong."

My father has always specialized in gifting me ways out, with escalating degrees of escape: I'd graduated from a T pass to a trip to an island that just barely existed.

The police called me back in three more times. It was soon clear that they had nothing concrete on me. The questions remained the same, and the last session was purely perfunctory, a farewell tour of the station whose weak tea I was growing to enjoy, yet another routine into which I could throw myself.

The waning of the authorities' interest correlated with the complete absence of suspects. It slipped out on my last visit that Ayale's whereabouts were unknown, as were those of their source: somehow, through some channel that the police had failed to observe, they'd disappeared, and the cops' frantic attempts to locate them were for naught. The disciples were fragmented, useless, becoming invisible. Food lost what little taste it had left.

The time immediately preceding our departure was notable only for a marked increase in stasis. I slept as much as my body would let me and consumed as little as would allow me to sleep. It was a time of complete peace between my father and me: we'd reached an understanding.

Sunday brunch was recommenced. My father said things like this preserved our humanity, and I understood what he meant enough to go along with it.

One morning he left. I didn't understand his certainty, but I obediently defrosted the refrigerator, broke the lease, dragged all of our furniture onto the sidewalk, and waited for a sign that I was to follow. Our landlord was only too glad to be rid of us, sick of our delayed rent and the police presence that he suspected was our doing.

We'd been receiving letters from a million people named Anonymous. They were either excruciatingly detailed or almost insultingly brief. The former enumerated the reasons I was a horrible person and inquired as to how I could live with myself. They invited me to peruse the enclosed lists of plagues that God would soon visit upon me, my family, and my progeny.

The latter wished only that God would forgive me, because they surely wouldn't.

These notes continued until the day I left for B——. I wonder if new ones keep arriving, piling up on the doorstep that is no longer ours. I wonder if our landlord has finally read some and, if he has, what he thinks it's all about.

When I arrived on B——, I felt as though I'd forgotten to do or bring something crucial, how one might feel after leaving the oven on, the door open, a wallet full of hundreds on the unmade bed. I think now that it was really Boston I left behind—or, rather, the version of Boston that contained the version of me to which I'd grown so accustomed.

We are nearly returned to the beginning now. I have nearly nothing more to say.

Part III: On the Subject of Revelations That Mean Less Than One Would Expect

It's been a long time since we've spoken at length to anyone. There's little to say. The excitement of the beginning, as remembered by the original settlers, has faded by our second month. We have as little idea of what happens next as we do what's happening now, and are no better informed as to how we're involved in either phase. The last few morning reports state only: all is as usual. These pronouncements intractably cement our suspension; I've even begun to notice—or perhaps it's my imagination—that the children are no longer growing, taking on new characteristics, trying out new phrases and gestures. When I give one of them a snack or bat their hands away from a sharp object, it's always the same apple I offered yesterday and the day before, it's the same gesture to remove the same limb from the same surface, which never ceases to be at that degree of sharpness and in that precise location of that specific room. We have become trapped on a mechanized track, which, as we sleep, tugs us back to where we began.

Many don't understand what we're all waiting so expectantly for, and still they wait. They've gathered from the murmurs that we're bounding forward to a new world, one of our own choosing, even though most of us weren't consulted during the process. The reasons for this endeavor, the potential consequences, the very real current effects escape them, hold no interest for them, or imply something so disquieting that they've decided, perhaps wisely, to cease investigating; the answers might be too horrifying to live with.

My free time has become excruciatingly plentiful: the children barely move anymore, there's no need to even halfheartedly chase them like in the dubiously happier days, and we stopped playing travel and betting on three-legged races a long time ago. Our hearts just aren't in it anymore.

When I started asking about the Danga, my father questioned if I was thinking of joining their illustrious ranks. He made like this was a joke, putting on what I imagined *he* imagined to be a teasing tone of voice. Living in such close quarters with him has enabled me to instantly recognize where he is on his emotional barometer. His only admission of feeling something other than blind good humor came in our first and only conversation about the Danga.

"Have you asked the others? They've been here longer—they probably know more."

"But you're the only one who's been in the same room as them. The others say that's never happened before."

We hid more than we showed. His tone of polite interest belied a fright that ate away at his internal organs, a condition that our one doctor has diagnosed as stress. I didn't mention that what the others said was never spoken directly to me, that I gathered information from around corners and the stilted chatter of the children.

"Maybe you shouldn't ask them anymore."

"I haven't really. Like I said, you probably know more."

"Let's keep it like that."

"That's what I've been doing."

"I know. But sometimes I like to repeat things I've already told you."

"Why?"

"Because I'm becoming an old man and that's what old men do—they ask the same questions and give the same answers and warn you of the same dangers, even if those dangers no longer exist."

"If you know all that, couldn't you just put off getting old?"

Our banter masked what we were learning: he, that I would never ask the others for information; and I, that this was no longer an acceptable topic of conversation.

Going anywhere near the Danga headquarters is impossible without attracting attention, located as it is in an almost circular clearing, all vegetation apparently too scared to approach. My few spying missions have consisted of strolling past, pretending that I'm taking an improbably long route to our house. I once saw a dog in front of their residence, despite having been told that the island's last canine expired in 1975.

I'm not always sure why I care about the Danga as much as I do, but as this second month drags onward—and make no mistake, it's dragging itself along on the slowest and most stumbling of feet, since the invention of new worlds is thrilling only for those who are at the forefront of the creative process; those who shuffle through the paces of what has already been made are little better than pawns in a chess game, to use a tired metaphor, and why not, we are all tired—I persist in wondering who these people are, what they look like, who they were before they could show their faces only to each other. Maybe they were all members of the same family, like the seeds of a dynasty-to-be, or maybe there was a recruiting call for those who liked secrets and power. My recurring dreams involve colorful masks with exaggerated features, pulled off faces that look familiar before I forget them again. In an existence where everything has come to a bleary halt, they remain in sharp focus, making indiscernible movements toward definitive changes that I know must be taking place, even if I can't see them. In this way, I keep at bay the vague dread that plagues most of my fellows.

Although I am one of those with a visible face and visible motives and thus of no real interest, I feel closer to the Danga than to the others. I'm sure Ayale would joke that *of course* I've decided to ally myself with the ruling class, that if it was up to me, I'd be chief oligarch and have three chariots, with two more just to look at. The real joke, of course, in that painfully accurate way of eighteenth-century short stories, where the moral jabs at your ribs before you get your breath back from the dying swoon of the heroine, is that this describes no one more accurately than Ayale himself.

I've already considered the idea that he might be in the Danga, but I know it's not possible. Life doesn't make things like that possible anymore, not since the eighteenth century, not since people stopped writing about that kind of eighteenth century.

Our numbers have been steadily swelling, a subject on which the Danga just as steadily refuses to comment. The new arrivals go to great lengths to keep themselves apart. They cluster at one corner of the table during meals, they leave for work before daybreak, they cover the lower halves of their faces with scarves—because of the sand, some say; because they are Jews, whisper others—and yet the brief glimpses I've caught convince me that I was right all along. I'm not sure why or how, but the disciples are here. They're being sown into our midst, and my hair is falling out in greater clumps from the fear that clutches me in the morning and doesn't release me until I sleep. I couldn't get out of bed today, so constricted did my lungs feel, and my father timidly suggested that I smoke less.

I can handle some of this being my fault, but surely the rest can't be. Aren't I too young to have done so much wrong? Weren't my intentions no worse than any other person's? Didn't I usually donate a dollar for cancer research during supermarket credit card purchases? Didn't I genuinely hope that my dollar would be the one to eradicate the disease? But was that an egotistical desire? Did I do more harm than good with all those dollars? Did I do more harm than good with all those years?

Desta, whose left arm is shrunken—either from birth or a witch, depending on his level of sobriety—is the latest attendant on the island. I hid in our house this afternoon, letting the children play outside it, waiting for him to pass during his postlunch constitutional. When he was in front of the door, I lunged forward, accidentally kicking the youngest in the process.

"Why are you here?"

The little one sobbed as the middle child, the creator of words, stared at us, unblinking.

Desta didn't speak; he'd always had a soft spot for me. I dug my nails into his withered arm, simultaneously recoiling from the sensation of his skin against my hand.

"Where is he?"

The youngest continued to scream as I joined him in his

tears. Desta pried my fingers off, continued to the water, and didn't look back. It took hours to quiet the child.

Are the disciples here as a reward for them? Or as a punishment for us?

A moment of truth: we are all tired. We are fed up with palm trees, we weary of morning swims, we are indifferent to our effortless tans, five-star sunsets have become draining, we are worn out by a climate pattern that veers between heartbreaking serenity and enervating humidity. It's no longer fun to be woken up by the sun (we miss our alarm clocks); the novelty of the beach is long gone (we have rashes, and something is biting us between our toes). Our least favorite colors are turquoise and foam. We never did like seafood.

We no longer see the point of seven A.M. breakfasts and ten P.M. beddings. We have grown sick of our beds, their sizes, their shapes, their lack of softness, their lack of firmness, their inability to cradle us to sleep, their refusal to become more amenable to the shapes of our bodies, their failure to resemble the beds of our childhoods, the ones that kept us safe when our parents were working and the rest of the neighborhood didn't care. We are too harassed by our beds to sleep anymore. I have begun to doze off while looking after the children, only to wake in a panic; there are no sirens, no arguments from Sissy next door about how she *will* get her hair relaxed, her mother can go *fuck* her nigger ass. I am the most tired of crying.

We are bored by the Danga. We are bored by their repetitive squabbles over things we don't understand and don't care about because it's not like anyone's going to explain. They've become negligent about turning off the public address system, so that it's frequently on when it shouldn't be, and their words reverberate in the backgrounds of our lives.

"Let's take some of them now! How else will we know?"

"What more do you need to know? This wasn't what I thought—"

"If we're losing we should go, but if we're winning we should go *now*."

"I don't want to stay, I don't want to d—"

"What if he's wrong?"

The woman's voice is always absent from these strangled bits of exchange. We hear only men, bearing the meticulously trained Addis Ababa newscaster vocal rhythms, wherein emphases are placed in unlikely moments and the tone follows a brutal hills-and-valleys progression. I keep expecting someone to deliver an inaccurate weather report—hot today until it rains or maybe doesn't rain but stops being hot—or announce the abysmal scores of a soccer team. Bereft of the usual tics and accents which mark us as being from one locale as opposed to another, it turns out that the rest of the Danga is interchangeable, Ethiopian robots transplanted here by chance. It's doubtful whether their spokesperson would seem distinct if it wasn't for her being a woman and, thus, the most fundamental kind of different of all.

The rampant disagreement which roams their ranks bores us to tears. The suddenly copious morning pamphlets seem like deliberate insults to our intelligence, with their growing limitations on what is permitted in the realms of thought and action. Their delight in the cryptic is dull. We feel nothing when they invoke the name of Mengistu to show us how lucky we are to be building and living in this great new world. We are too tired to point out, even to each other, that if one has to gesture at a psychopathic murderer with delusions of grandeur to justify one's behavior, then maybe something has gone horribly wrong.

We are in the mood of missing hot foods; we don't care that it's too stifling to eat them. We miss *doro wet, siga wet, kitfo, lega tibs, awaze tibs, zelzel tibs, katenga* on weekend mornings with butter dripping onto the table because it's still *mitad* fresh, *shiro wet, minchet abish*, pasta with Parmesan, roast beef sandwiches with horseradish all over, deep-dish pizza, thin-crust pizza with barbecue sauce, the casseroles that our American friends served with reheated dinner rolls, Buffalo wings, dipping sauces all in a row, fried chicken and biscuits, hamburgers, steak fries, leftover apple pie from Thanksgiving that keeps through December.

We yearn for the sensation of cleaning in the singular, for the days when cleaning one bathroom was the achievement of the week. We've come to despise the sound of collective breathing over buckets of dirty water and dirtier rags. We abhor the sound of the sea as we scrub; it brings to mind a peace from which we have never been further. We dread the unavoidable bumping of elbows at meals, the inevitable spilling of something sticky on another person's flesh. Any illusions of solitude or privacy are just that, and nothing more: we can perpetually hear each other living.

We are no longer capable of entertaining ourselves with nothing more than ourselves. We have heard every single joke that every single one of us knows, including the one about the Irish bartender who buys a goat. We tried to write a play together, but stopped when it became about a group of people who are unhappy on an island. My father tried to revive our spirits by building a guitar and a trombone, but while both bore strong resemblances to those instruments, neither made a single musi-

cal kind of sound—a note, if you will—not even accidentally,
unless one counts the percussive potentials of banging them
against solid objects.

If we were going to put our cards on the table, we would
say that we're tired of waiting for the revolution. We're tired of
reassurances that we're doing something tremendous, one for
the books that our children will read, and the newspaper clip-
pings that they will proudly incorporate into school projects,
although all newspapers will belong to the state and defacing
one will be as offensive as burning money. It has not escaped
us that older generations must do all they can to improve the
lives of future ones, but we had believed ourselves to be the
future. We were under the impression that we were the owed
ones. We had not counted on this debt of service.

We no longer comprehend why we do the things we do. The
Danga has stopped delivering hopeful tidings about our progress in attaining the land that is to be our final home. It has
stopped giving us small "historical" anecdotes which prove that
this future land was always meant to belong to us. I have begun
to suspect that the reason outside reading material is forbidden has less to do with the Danga wanting us to begin anew
than with it wishing to compel us toward forgetfulness of why
we came here in the first place. My father doesn't say anything,
but I know he's troubled. He has stopped making things.

I've been having new dreams about Ayale. Each one features the same room, where a single note card has been placed
on the floor. It says something different every night: *He has a
slight limp. His ears are too big.* Upon waking, I sometimes can't
remember what was written on that night's card. I've begun
writing down the sentences, reading all of them together every
day: if the citizens of Macondo were able to recover language,
I should be more than equal to the task of recovering a single

man. This all-consuming project forces me toward a violent anger against my father, and so a new kind of silence between us gains depth, weight, permanence.

One of the younger settlers, a woman in her early thirties whose hair is graying at an alarming rate, pulled me aside after dinner last night and demanded I tell her everything: Who is Ayale? What does all this mean? I shook her off. Her insistent naïveté irritated me—how could one sum up all that was Ayale? My last thought before entering into the now familiar dream-scape was that none of us could ever fathom what was happening and why it mattered; you're either born understanding it all or you die serving those who do. I don't know which is worse.

For the past two weeks' worth of mornings, we've been made to understand that we're not ready. Our breakfast pamphlets recount stories from the France, England, and Italy of long ago, about peoples who rose up against unjust emperors, mob rule, lazy landowners who played card games by day, beat serfs by night, and ended up lynched in populist takeovers. We've been told of soldiers who followed beloved generals into the very pits of death, of sultans who had only to raise a finger for an army of thousands to be assembled at their bedsides before midday. We've been walked through the courage of Tewodros, the cunning of Menelik, the greatness that pumped through Ethiopia's blood, even when she was a mere collage of king-doms. Compared to these stories and many others besides—we can't read all day; there are houses to clean, children to watch, seconds-minutes-half hours to count off—we've not shown ourselves worthy of the chance for greatness that the present is practically begging us to seize.

None of us disagrees. We'd be the first to admit that we

have nothing comparable to this fatalistic energy. While some mourn this lack, I can't help but see it as a sign of our superior intelligence. One can extoll the exploits of yore, but perhaps if it hadn't been so simple to declare war and run with it for these foolhardy emperors, gambling with their lives and those of their loyal subjects, we wouldn't be in this mess. I oppose loyalty when the one I'm supposed to be loyal to doesn't give two fucks about what might become of me. I've changed, you see.

The last few pamphlets have expressed thanks for our efforts, coupled with the reiteration of the belief that we can do better. We're no longer allowed to dispose of these morning texts after reading them; they will be included in an indestructible time capsule, to be buried in the earth of our new land. My father is feverishly compiling lists of needed alloys and other materials. He seems to be thriving again, for which I'm grateful.

Smoking had always been tolerated by the Danga. The workers bought cigarettes in town and distributed them during dinner, while my father left my pack under my pillow. Then a new injunction mandated that all smoking take place at least half a mile outside the settlement grounds, no more than two people at a time. Immediately on its heels came the news that smoking would no longer be allowed, period. Quite a few of the women gave me triumphant glances. I'm the only female who smokes in a culture where a woman who publicly brandishes a cigarette is basically a whore. This is where the remoteness of our house comes in handy, so that we can smoke at night, out the northwest windows, with no one the wiser. I told my father that if the Danga knew how essential tobacco was to his state of mind, they might make an exception for him.

There is a fear in the air that stinks up the place, stronger even than the ginger which befuddles my brain. It emanates directly from the invisible chambers of the Danga. The silence of the loudspeaker weighs heavy. On more than one occasion this week, I've walked into an area where I heard "Ayale . . ." before everyone saw me and went mute. I wonder if he is thought to be the reason for our present state or the only possible solution.

—

Yesterday, I refused to take care of the children. Yesterday, I demanded that my father let me leave. Today, a letter was nailed to our door.

"Sunrise tomorrow. Just the girl."

It was almost a relief.

After dinner, my father made coffee at home—he wouldn't reveal how he'd procured the materials—and when we drank it at midnight, all windows and doors closed, it tasted like the revolution that the Danga's been shoving down our throats. He noted, "Night coffee is sometimes how change begins," and I laughed because I knew what he meant and also because he'd said it like his business was transformation when, in fact, he was the kind of person who complained if there was no bow-tie pasta on Wednesdays, because that's what he always had. The coffee was strong and I was still awake right before sunrise, when two of the brightest stars I'd ever seen approached each other above my window. I woke my father and he said they were planets, silly. It's rare to hear him sound smug, and this made me happy: change was starting already.

—

I heard a story yesterday; the teller in the other room hadn't seen me.

Once upon a time, there was a woman who owned a tiny store in Dire Dawa; she was one of the first women to do so, and no one, including her, ever forgot it. One day, a man came and cheated her out of some money. Or took one of the umbrellas she was selling. Or swiped a few pieces of candy. She demanded restitution. The man refused. She insisted. The man fled to the capital. She left her children with her sister (who had never been named, because by the time her mother had noticed, it was easier to give orders to someone without one), closed the shop, and followed the man into the city. He ran to the other side of it. She raged forward as well, every minute spent away from her store losing her more money than anything he could have cost her.

It was in this way that she finally visited Axum and Gondar, and saw the people who put disks in their lips and earlobes to make them dangle and were as black as real Africans. After a year, the man grew tired. She didn't, so she found him and dragged him to court. In those days, the country was smaller and cared more, so everyone had heard about this cross-country cat-and-mouse chase. The judge agreed that the man had wronged her. (Everyone in the courtroom sighed. This was why he earned more money than all of them combined? To be the town crier of the obvious? To look at something and say that it *was* that something? The judge became nervous.)

"And I sentence him to jail for a year."

"No. Death."

This was from the woman, who didn't need a lawyer because she said she didn't.

"What?"

"Death. Put him to death."

"But surely this crime doesn't warrant—"

"If you don't do it, I will."

Everyone knew she would. Probably with her teeth.

The judge was beginning to sweat.

"All right."

"In front of me."

"What?"

"Kill him while I watch."

The judge fell off his chair. As in literally: he was sitting upright one minute and then was on the floor the next.

"Ma'am . . . for a woman . . . to, to . . ."

The woman stared. The judge summoned a flunky dressed in a khaki uniform (who may or may not have been an employee of the court, since at that time the cheapest form of dress was khaki attire) and whispered something to him. Within an hour, the man (who had spent the entire trial looking straight ahead, expressionless, having already accepted what he'd known from the start: that the minute he stopped, it was all over; redemption was in movement alone) was swinging from a tree near the courtroom. The woman calmly surveyed the scene, nodded once, twice, three times (a lady?) and then went home, where her children, having heard the tales about their mother, were frightened of her, a condition that would bleed into their children and those children's children until the first of them finally left for America.

This woman, concluded the speaker, was Ayale's mother.

I was squinting into the direction I thought might be east, trying to decide if this qualified as full sunrise when the door behind me opened. I walked in, turned around, and saw my mother for the first time in twelve years. She had aged profoundly. I drew as close to her as I dared and opened my arms, which she neatly sidestepped to move to another door on the opposite side of the room.

"You must be hungry," she called.

She returned with a loaf of bread and a knife.

"Do you have any coffee?"

She left and came back with a full pot.

"What are you doing here?" I asked.

"I work here."

Her last words replayed in my mind.

"You're the voice on the loudspeaker."

"I didn't think you'd remember my voice after so many years."

"I didn't, either."

"Do you want sugar in your coffee?"

"How long have you known that I was here?"

"I told your father how to find us."

"What?"

She sliced the bread. I'm tired of people not answering, forcing me to find responses to my own questions. Some might call this true knowledge, teaching someone how to fish as opposed to just handing over some mackerel, but I hate that expression and the process is exhausting.

"Were you the one he was seeing on the weekends?"

"I wasn't there. I'd send things to a mailbox and he'd pick them up."

"The shirt? That was you?"

"Yes!" She was pleased. "Did you like it?"

"Why didn't you ever come see me?"

"There was never a good time. Did you like it? That's one of my favorite colors."

"And yet you had plenty of time to send all that shit."

"Please don't swear. Have some bread."

"I'm not hungry."

She maintained her silence until I took a slice.

"You've gotten so thin."

"Why am I here?"

She took a visibly deep breath.

"I have to go back a bit."

"Go right ahead. I've canceled my other appointments."

"Thank you."

Another breath. Her hairline was receding. Nothing should have led to this.

"Around the time your father started to visit us—those horrible visits!—I was beginning to panic. We were living off an advance from the house-sitting job. I had nothing else lined up. I couldn't take you to interviews, and I couldn't afford babysitters; I only found that job because of the nice cashier at Star Market."

"Gloria."

I had forgotten her of the Technicolor braids.

"It was stressful. You were too young then, but maybe now you can understand what a simultaneous lack of money and love can do to a person."

"I loved you."

"It wasn't enough. Forgive me, but it wasn't enough."

She left and came back with another cup. When she was done pouring coffee, she continued.

"I don't know how he heard of me, but one morning, Ayale was on our doorstep, all smiles and muffins. I invited him in. You were still asleep. We sat at the kitchen table, he introduced himself, then launched into how he'd heard that I was having some trouble and he wanted to help. I asked him why, and he said because all who are exiled must stick together."

"How poetic."

"He saved our lives. He gave me two hundred dollars and made me promise to come see him when we were back in Boston. I couldn't wait that long. As soon as it seemed like your father was serious about returning, I took the first train back. I was fascinated by the man."

"Were you in love with him?"

She looked at me and then swiftly away.

"It was never a factor."

"Did he ever see me when I was a child?"

"No, I don't believe so."

"Did he ever hear my name?"

"I don't think so."

"Go on."

The more coffee I drank, the more drained I felt.

"I went to the address he'd given me, which turned out to be a parking lot. He took me to lunch and, well, he just made so much *sense*. Why *shouldn't* we change the world? He asked me about you, and I said that you were taken care of. In that case, he said, you can start right away. I began traveling around trying to spread word of our project, kind of like what Father was doing. Then he called me back to Boston. The test run was in full force, but they needed local governors; he asked if I was interested."

"So, let's review: you came back to Boston. And still didn't see me. In Boston. Where I lived."

She remained calm.

"I understand your anger."

"Were you the one who kept calling?"

She nodded.

"I would wait until the others were asleep. Ayale gave me your number."

"Why did he choose you?"

"He said he had a good feeling about it. The rest of the Danga had already been selected, but it was all men. He felt it would be better to have at least one female representative."

Her tone didn't match the sudden redness of her face, the shaking of her hands. She laughed, a cutting and cut-off sound.

"No other woman would have said yes. I had nothing to lose; I had no one else."

"What about me? You had me."

"When I complained that this hadn't been in the job description, I couldn't take it anymore, that monster tried to convince me that without my personal . . . attentions, there would be a bloodbath, too much unrelieved tension. I asked him if continual rape was the only solution he could envision. He said he felt that was the wrong word to use. I said I would leave. He asked me how I planned on doing that. Then he said: You are where you are because I put you there; you will stay until I put you somewhere else."

I tried to hug her but, when she withdrew, took her hands instead.

"When your father told me how close you and Ayale were becoming, I threatened to shoot him if he didn't drag you two apart. True to form, he failed."

"You can't force anyone to do anything."

"How comforting."

"Why am I here?"

Changing the subject is a key maneuver to learn, take it from me.

She touched me for the first time, her right hand on my shoulder. Her eyes were the same shape as mine.

"Do you mind if I smoke?"

I had already lit a cigarette.

"Didn't we outlaw that?"

"Just answer me. And don't get my father into trouble for the cigarettes—that's my fault, too."

"I thought things would be fine after you left for college,

but I'd underestimated Ayale. Once the idea got into everyone's head that it was you who had turned him in and forced him to flee, I knew you'd never be safe if you stayed in America. He has an enormous network of spies and contacts. They would have killed you."

She checked to see that I was conscious before she continued.

"You needed to disappear. I spoke to Father, and he spread the rumor that you and your father were always meant to move here. The police, Ayale's premature departure from Boston—it was all part of the plan. If someone didn't understand, it was because they weren't meant to."

"I can tell that you're very proud of yourself."

"I'm sorry. This is a lot."

"Oh no, I get this all the time. I thought you were going to tell me something crazy."

"Please sit down."

"My father told me a year. Can we go after a year?"

She didn't have to speak; her face told me how stupid I was, to not know that I was trapped.

"Out of curiosity, was this why I was asked to come this morning?"

"I'm afraid not."

I lay down across the floor, forehead smashed into the frigid concrete.

"Tell me."

She took one of her deep breaths.

"Perhaps you've noticed a few additions to our community."

"Ye-e-e-s."

I dragged out the word to prolong the time before her next sentence.

"We—the Danga—have been meeting with these men. We

thought they might be here to prepare us for Ayale's arrival or our evacuation."

My heart dropped to my feet and then careened back up again.

"Is he here?"

She shook her head.

"They've been sent by him. It seems that he's decided to launch events a bit differently."

"I don't understand."

"Financially, we're finished. The men are here to help us move."

"So wait—we're going? He won?"

Her discomfort was palpable.

"The land isn't in our hands yet, but if we stay, we run the risk of losing our investors, once they see how hopeless our position is. I don't know where we're going. All I know is that the Danga won't be in charge anymore; Ayale will take over."

Despite myself, my spirits surged, which didn't go unnoticed.

"There are caveats," she cautioned. "Conditions."

"I know what a caveat is."

"You and your father will not be coming with us."

"What do you even—"

"Ayale feels that you are both completely ill-prepared for the mission."

"So what does he expect us to do? Where are we supposed to go?" I was sitting upright now.

Her eyes had roamed to a point slightly to the right of me. She cleared her throat.

"Well?"

"Your father can do as he wants, but you're now an active danger."

Her eyes were brimming over.

"What's going to happen to me?"

She knelt and brought her hands up as if to cup my face, but then thought better of it.

"You are to be put to death in two weeks' time."

Her perfume smelled famous.

"I'm still your daughter! You could convince them!"

I went quiet when I thought about what it might take to persuade the men of the Danga.

"I've already tried. I volunteered to escort you to whatever location he chose, but he wouldn't have it."

She stood back up, adjusting invisible things on her knees.

"The Danga only let you in because I begged and everyone thought it was what Ayale wanted."

I considered this.

"What will happen to you? Does he know that you and Father helped us?"

This time she looked me directly in the eyes.

"I hope not."

"But if he does?"

"You don't need me to tell you; you're a big girl."

I collapsed onto the floor, eyes trained on the ceiling, not sure how to find my cigarettes from this position.

"It'll be a firing squad. Compulsory attendance for everyone."

I rose and silently closed the door behind myself as she wept. It turns out that it's quite a simple thing, leaving: no wonder all the adults I know keep doing it, without a backward glance.

As soon as my father arrived home that night, I started talking and didn't stop until it felt as though all the words I knew had been sucked out. To his credit, he listened to everything, with no interruptions. When he asked to hear the story again, he was just as attentive. When I'd finished, he stared at the wall behind me. We smoked awhile before I spoke.

"After we arrived on the island, did you still communicate with her?"

"No. That was one of her stipulations."

"What were the others?"

"I couldn't tell you or anyone that I knew her. I had to accept any subsequent decision the Danga made regarding us, with the understanding that she wouldn't intercede. You shouldn't have left her like that."

"I know."

Quiet again, until he cleared his throat.

"This might be a stupid question but . . . how do you feel?"

"Not real. I don't believe any of this is going to happen."

"Maybe it doesn't have to."

"I don't think you're really grasping the concept of a death sentence."

"You won't want to hear this, but your mother's been trying to save you from the moment you came back into her life. She brought you here. She just gave you two weeks' advance notice; when has the Danga ever given fair warning? Do you think any-one will do the same for her if he decides to get rid of her?"

I stared at him, and he nodded.

"I'd bet money that she's almost died for your sake on more than one occasion."

I remembered how small she'd looked, how I'd left her to cry alone, and knew that the break inside me was for forever. He tried to smile.

"You'll have to head out early, when it's still dark. I'll steal as much food as I can for you, and I'll draw you a map to the phone I used when I got here. It's a long walk, so you'll have to move fast before you get too hungry. There are plenty of tourists around that area. I remember them, all wearing those long shorts; find someone who can help you."

"They'll just kill me sooner."

"Leave it to me." He pointed to my bed. "Now get some sleep."

I rolled in, relishing the prospect of hours of unconsciousness in the face of imminent freefall. Suddenly, he wrapped his arms around my prone body.

"I know you don't think much of us as parents, and maybe it's in the nature of being a teenager to think that no one has suffered as greatly as you, but you're right, we've been lousy as lousy can be. Still, I want you to remember that while we weren't there for a lot of small things, we really have been trying to make up for it with the big things. Will you remember that?" I nodded into my pillow. "Good."

He released me, and I heard the sound of his feet on the floor, approaching his own bed. When I woke up the next morning, the sun was high, and he was nowhere in sight.

My father arrived home an hour ago with two bananas and four slices of bread for my meager store. He tells me to get ready to leave tonight; I will know when. Before I go to bed I hug him, something I haven't done in years. He smiles and playfully tugs my hair. I assume that his plan includes his escape as well as mine, perhaps the two of us acting as decoys for each other. This makes sense so long as I don't think too hard about it.

I wake up in the middle of the night because I hear a crash. By the time I light a candle, my father's body, strung up from the strongest beam of the ceiling, has already ceased to struggle. The stool falling when he kicked it away was what had roused me. I run outside and scream until the others begin to arrive, the first being our nearest neighbor, who joins me in my shrill alarm when she sees what has happened. It seems like only seconds before the house is filled with bodies, shrieking, and melting candle wax. I had already slung my bag onto my back when I released the first cry and I'd slept in my regular clothes, both facts thankfully concealed by the dark. As the mayhem skyrockets, I slip around back, in the direction indicated on my father's map. I run so fast that it's only upon colliding with a tree that I realize I haven't stopped crying since I first opened my eyes.

All I want to do is crumple and sleep until my wretched breathing goes away, but as self-indulgent as I am, even I can't justify wasting the embarrassment of life bestowed upon me by my parents. I've been advancing at the same rate all morning, stopping only when my tears obscure my vision and I must blot them away. They are of sadness but also fury. I feel invincible, which, it turns out, is a horrible thing to feel: I have never been less human.

The more of B—— I see, the more I'm struck by its outstanding beauty. I wish that my father and I had taken vacations together. Even my mother and I stayed by the ocean once, in a house that wasn't our own, which is kind of like a hotel.

I sometimes wish I'd never met Ayale, but more often I think that meeting him was the first real thing that happened in my life. Perhaps I'm growing up, but the process is killing me.

All throughout the last month, I wanted my father to wake up in the middle of the night. I thought it would help me feel less lonely. I tried to will him awake. I once pushed him. Nothing worked. His snores seemed to increase in volume and frequency, keeping me awake even longer.

I'm smoking now and hoping that someone will either see my smoke and give me food or see it and shoot me. I'm exhausted, I'm starving, I ate a rotten banana and it's giving me terrible daydreams and breath, I miss my father, I want someone to save me, I want someone to tell me where to go and what to do and I will do it, I will do it with the pleasure of not thinking.

Also, I keep hearing noises from behind me but no one's ever there.

I'm just being paranoid. It's the trauma, don't you know.

The breathing I hear, which is definitely not my own, doesn't exist. It couldn't. This is a trick my mind is playing on me, to deceive me into thinking that I'm not just flung out here on my own devices. It's not working, though, because what my mind is forgetting is that it's mine, and so I'm using it to play games with itself twice as quickly and twice as hard as it's attempting to pull a fast one on me.

My biggest fear is that I'll go crazy. Scratch that. My biggest fear is that I will never have food again, but going crazy is a close second.

I can hear the breathing again, and all of a sudden, that feels really good. I don't want to start pulling theories out of my ass this late in the game, but if Ayale really *is* on his way here, and that really *is* him behind me, this could be my chance to talk to him, make him realize just how mistaken he is, maybe even tell him about my father.

Or maybe he'll just slaughter me here, where there are no witnesses, and never think about me again.

Also, wouldn't Ayale just send a disciple? Personalized execution is for those who matter.

I checked again and no one's there, but I always thought Ayale could hide with the best of them. Call it instinct.

Go to college, kids! If not, you'll literally die alone!

If my heart beats any faster, cardiac arrest will be the end of me because I'm no hummingbird and my heart is meant to be measured in its pace.

I'm going to turn around, just one last time.

No I won't! I must be losing so many kilowatts of energy every time I turn my neck.

I just did it. Science was never my subject of choice.

No one's there.

I keep thinking of Odysseus telling the Cyclops that his name is Nobody and getting away but then ruining it by boasting that his name is Odysseus, bam, take that Polyphemus. I hated Odysseus. I hate overly clever men.

One more turn around and then I'm done.

It would be terrible and hilarious if, after all this, it was a heart attack that finished me. I survived the firing squad, but my eighteen-year-old heart failed me.

Just one more and then it's eyes forward for the rest of this stroll.

No one there.

I need to move on. Make something of myself. Meet some new people.

Once more.

Not there.

Good. Good, good, good.

What if I can't make anything of myself? Without him, I would have been just another example of boring and slight upward mobility. I would have been just me.

He's still not there.

At least I'm not a prick like Odysseus. But also, he had adventures.

No one is coming for me, not to save me, not to kill me, because I'm not worth the effort.

I guess my father thought I was worth the effort. I guess he thought it all along. My mother too, in her own way, after a while.

Still no one.

I really loved him. I really loved her. I really loved all of them.

One more turn.

There is nothing now that I don't miss about before.

Acknowledgments

Massive and heartfelt thanks to:

my family, who even when they didn't get it, loved me enough to pretend until they did; my friends, who have become family, and who cooked for me, traveled with me, read my drafts, and advised me through visas, tax returns, real estate, emotions; Victor LaValle, who gave me shit until I got better, and then gave me my chance; my agent, Julia Masnik, who stuck with me and believed in me, even when I didn't; my editor, Caroline Zancan, who championed this book when many wouldn't; and Kevstar, who has done all of these things and more, despite my whining.

About the Author

Nafkote Tamirat is a native of Boston. She holds
an MFA from Columbia University. Her short stories
have appeared in *Birkensnake, The Anemone Sidecar*,
and *Best Paris Stories. The Parking Lot Attendant* is
her first novel.

Black Mountain Public Library
105 Dougherty St.
Black Mountain, NC 28711